A Taste
of the
Twenties

A Taste

of the

Twenties

The Back Inn Time Series
Book Six

Stephenia H. McGee

By The
Vine Press

A Taste of the Twenties
Published by: By The Vine Press, LLC
www.StepheniaMcGee.com

Printed in the United States of America

Cover design: Roseanna White Designs
Other images used under license.

Library of Congress Cataloging-in-Publication Data
Names: McGee, Stephenia H. (Stephenia H. McGee) 1983 –
Title: A Taste of the Twenties / Stephenia H. McGee
240p. 5 in. x 8in.
Description: By The Vine Press digital eBook edition | By The Vine Press Trade paperback edition | Mississippi: By The Vine Press, 2024
Summary: Meeting your heroes from the past is awesome. Unless you get stuck with them forever.
Identifiers: ISBN-13: 978-1-63564-096-0 (trade)
Subjects: Christian Historical Fiction | Time Travel Romance | Romantic Comedy

Dear reader,

As a historical fiction writer, I've always wondered what it would be like if I could travel back in time and get a firsthand glimpse of the eras I love to read about. Thus, the idea for this series was born. It's a fun way to imagine the impossible.

Please keep in mind, dear reader, that a story is all this is meant to be. It is not meant to spark a theological debate on whether God would allow the miracle of time travel. The Bible tells us "Man's days are determined; You [God] have decreed the number of his months and have set limits he cannot exceed" (Job 14:5) and "My times are in your hands" (Psalm 31:15).

Several of the things regarding the time travel in this story are not possible, but it allows us to suspend what we know to be true to simply enjoy the fictional freedom of the what if...? So, come with me, imaginative reader, and together let's go see what it might be like to "step back inn time and leave our troubles behind"!

Happy reading!
Stephenia

One

No. Oh no. Amelia Cabrera flung her dish towel over her shoulder and fought against the bile boiling up her throat. This couldn't be happening. If she ruined Chef's espagnole she'd be toast for sure.

She jammed a spoon into the brown mixture, and her stomach dropped. Too thick. Had she really left the heat that high? She could have bet her toque hat she'd reduced it to simmer—something that took at least an hour—before turning to other duties. Lowering the heat now did no good. Browned bits clung to the bottom of the pan, and the smell wrinkled her nose, overpowering the other aromas of Chef Dubois's delicacies coating the bustling kitchen.

Maybe if she thinned it out with a little water. Biting her lip between her teeth and flinging a prayer heavenward for a miracle, she drizzled a few tablespoons of tepid water into the sauce. She needed this job. The rent in Atlanta was high enough to make a girl almost starve. She was already behind on the weekly amount she paid her roommate for the closet-sized space she crashed into in the wee morning hours. If she didn't perform well enough in her two-week trial to land this position, she'd be out of cash and—

She shoved thoughts of rent to the back burner. No time for that now.

Pots clanged, and sous chefs clamored to one another as the kitchen ramped up for the busiest time of the evening. Their customers would settle into tables they'd reserved weeks in advance, ready for a night of culinary perfection. Amelia whipped her whisk through the concoction, but the lost cause defied her with unappealing lumps.

What else could she do? Broth, maybe? If she dug out the burnt bits and strained the lumps, then maybe she could put enough stock in to salvage most of it. It would be less than the regular batch and would take longer than planned, but anything was better than starting over. At least she hadn't yet added the truffles. She could pay a month's rent for what those things cost.

"And here I thought you were a *saucier*." Nadine's snide voice cut into Amelia's panicked whisking and sent a cold tingle along her arms.

Where was that strainer? She couldn't risk disrupting the orchestrated masterpiece of beef tenderloin with truffle and shallot demi-glace. She pursed her lips at the mess. Hopefully no one would order the most popular dish in the restaurant for the first hour of the evening.

"And is this all you made?" Nadine leaned over the pan and sniffed. "Hardly enough, even before you ruined it."

Amelia watched her stride away. Commenting wouldn't do any good anyway. In the grand total of twelve days she'd worked in the La Petite Fleur, she'd somehow managed to make the blond her enemy. Now she only had two days left to earn Chef's respect. She didn't have time to worry over why someone disliked her.

Setting the pan aside to strain once it cooled, she snagged another from the hook overhead and gathered her ingredients. A rich stock she'd simmered yesterday, butter, and flour. Would she need to chop a new mirepoix? Chef would notice for sure if she set to chopping a new batch of the onion, celery, and carrot mixture. What tricks could she use to speed up the process? She collected the tomato puree and the sachet of herbs.

She'd have to make a quick new roux and simmer it with stock. Then mix in the strained sauce and use it to deepen the flavors. If she pushed the heat to the highest simmer possible...maybe. Sweat gathered in her hairline and trickled down the back of her neck.

Rushing could give her nothing more than a large batch that might as well dance off the spoon and yell "amateur!"

Mamá's advice squirmed into her thoughts. *Better right than rushed,* mijita. *Time and care make for the best results.*

The memory of Papá's gentle hands guiding hers through their family recipes brought a tight pinch, and she had to make herself tuck it away for another time.

"Cabrera!"

Her whisk clattered to the floor. She let the mess drip off her tennis shoe and snatched another utensil. She couldn't risk ruining the roux. Not even to face Chef properly.

"Yes, sir?" She worked the tool through the sauce with shaking fingers.

Chef prodded the contents of the discarded pan. "What happened?"

Heat broiled up her neck, and she renewed her vigorous whisking. "I thought I turned it to simmer, but I guess..." Lame. Totally lame. There was no excuse for overheating.

"Hmm." He lifted a spoonful to his nose. "Shame. Could have been a good batch."

Her stomach twisted at his disappointment.

"This is the third offense in as many days, Cabrera."

The knot cinched tighter. "Sorry, Chef."

"And you had such high marks." He plopped the spoon into the pan and splattered brown liquid across the stove. He shooed her from her task.

She yielded her overworked whisk and stepped back to wring her hands. Would he yell at her? Dismiss her? That knot threatened to eject her meager lunch. No way. She forced the feeling down. She would *not* get sick in the kitchen.

"There is talent here." He tapped the whisk on the edge of the pan. "Just not enough."

The knot deflated and her knees weakened. She clutched the stainless-steel counter before he could notice.

"Come back in a few years, *oui*? When you have settled that nervous streak and can be more reliable."

"But, Chef, I—"

"Nadine!" The name cut through the clamor and settled every gaze on Amelia's humiliation.

The thirtysomething woman sidled over in a perfectly clean jacket. "Yes, Chef?"

He waved a hand at Amelia's station. "Fix this."

"Of course."

As she twisted the handle to reposition the pan, Amelia could have sworn a victorious turn slid over Nadine's lips.

Wait. Hadn't Nadine stopped by to look at her sauce about twenty minutes ago? Surely, she hadn't adjusted the temperature. No. That would be...

Amelia's fists tightened. Yesterday when her hollandaise broke, hadn't Nadine been there handing her the butter? She'd thought maybe they'd been reaching a working relationship. But what if she'd been sabotaging her?

"Did you turn up the heat on my sauce?" The words fired between her lips before she could capture them.

Nadine rolled her eyes. "Fumbling to place blame for your failures? How unbecoming. Not to mention entirely unprofessional." She rolled the spoon around the edge of the pan, not meeting Amelia's gaze. "Look, it's a tough business. Not many are cut out for it. Perhaps you should go home to your family's restaurant and make some simpler, ethnic dishes. I'm sure you'll be much happier there where you belong, instead of an upscale place like this."

Amelia's jaw slackened. She'd coated every word with honey, but the thick layer of cyanide underneath soured her mouth. "Excuse me?"

"Best collect your things, dear. If Chef notices you hanging around his kitchen past your welcome, it won't be pretty."

6

"How dare you!" Amelia ripped the spoon from Nadine's hand. "You think I'm going to tuck tail and run because you don't like me? What reason you could have, God only knows. But I worked too hard to land this job to let you steal it from me."

Something tickled between her ears over the pounding of her pulse. It took a moment to register the sound.

Silence.

No clattering pots. No shouted orders or calls for ingredients.

Amelia puffed out her cheeks and faced her audience. Everyone stared at her. She clenched her teeth and found the one pair of eyes she dreaded most.

Chef stalked her way. What felt like a gallon of popping candy fizzed in her stomach, but she notched her chin higher and locked her gaze on his. He opened his mouth.

Now or never.

Amelia pointed the spoon at her adversary. "She's been sabotaging me. She turned the heat up on my sauce when I wasn't looking, and yesterday, she...she..." What could Nadine have done with the butter? Slipped in too much when she wasn't looking?

Chef's focus swung to Nadine, who stirred Amelia's espagnole. "Explain."

Nadine lifted her shoulder. "The child is distraught and searching for excuses. What possible reason could I have to take an interest in a newbie?"

What possible reason? Maybe because Amelia had graduated at the top of her class at NOCHI—New Orleans Culinary and Hospitality Institute—or because she'd been the youngest sous chef ever invited to intern at La Petite Fleur. Who knew? Maybe the woman felt threatened.

"I will not suffer drama in my kitchen." Chef clapped his hands, making the other gawking sous chefs jump. They turned back to their tasks with renewed vigor. "Miss Cabrera."

Miss? Not a good sign. "But, Chef, if you'll let me explain."

He held up a hand. "Another word and my good faith offer for you to return when you've had a little time to grow up will expire."

She snapped her teeth together. Grow up? She was twenty-three! As Nadine's lips curled, Amelia fought against the urge to bonk her over the head with the dripping spoon she clutched between white knuckles.

"Take your leave before you make it worse, oui?" He thrust his chin toward the rear door where the chefs left their personal effects.

Her mouth might as well have been stuffed with a dozen persimmons. Her best shot at becoming an executive chef in this city turned on his heel and strode away as though he hadn't just shattered her dreams.

Nadine leaned over the sauce and inhaled slowly.

Amelia clutched her spoon like a guide wire. The only thing between her and a fall into misery. Except it didn't do her any good.

Mustering every shred of dignity she could scrape from her core, she deposited the spoon on the stainless-steel counter and wiped her hands down her jacket, leaving brown smears.

Little needles pricked behind her eyes, but she wouldn't cry. Would not. She gathered her purse and keys and slipped into the dark alley. She fingered her phone for several heartbeats before connecting to the person she most hated to disappoint.

Her mother answered on the third ring.

"Mamá?" Her throat constricted.

"Oh, mijita. What's wrong?"

"I–I have to come home." No words had ever tasted so sour.

Two

Top of the seventh. Two outs. Two to three count. A no-hitter on the line. Nolan Reed positioned his feet on the mound and leaned into the stretch. Third game of spring training and he was making good on his chance to play with the major-league starters. Sweat trickled down the back of his neck as he locked eyes with Fitzgerald, another AA guy who got a chance to show his stuff today in front of a crowd in Phoenix.

He twisted the ball in his glove, fingers caressing the stitches. Deep breath. The hubbub dimmed. His focus honed. He forgot the heat of the Arizona sun, the scent of dust in his nose. All that mattered now was the pitch with the nasty drop their lineup hadn't been able to hit.

One more throw and he'd retire another batter.

The catcher's mitt loomed. Impossible to miss today. He pulled into the windup, rocking his weight onto his right leg. He gripped the ball, ready to let his sinker rip. The Ranger bobbed his bat. The umpire settled into position.

This was it. The pitch to make his splash.

Knee up. Weight shift. He propelled all his six-three frame down the mound, slinging every ounce of his body into the throw. His arm came forward.

Pain rocketed through his elbow and up his triceps and exploded behind his eyes. The ball came free. He dropped his glove and sank to his knees, vision blurring.

The crack of the bat registered between the pulsing in his ears. Nolan gripped his elbow and forced himself to his feet.

Fitzgerald tossed the bat and started toward first.

"Reed!" The trainer's voice punched through the fog coating his brain, and the pain surged anew.

He grunted in response. Just needed to shake it off. He'd lost the no-hitter, but he still had time to salvage this inning. He released his elbow and let his hand drop. His stomach went with it. Despite his best efforts, the pain must have been obvious.

Martin gestured to the manager, and he approached with a grim set to his lips.

No. They couldn't take him out. Not yet.

"I'm fine, Martin. Just give me a sec." Nolan risked a glance at his elbow, then tried to turn the bruising flesh away from the trainer's view.

No such luck.

"Looks like an olecranon fracture. You'll need at least an X-ray. Maybe an MRI." Martin waved him off the mound.

A hush settled on the crowd, and even though he knew they couldn't hear him from here, he lowered his voice. "It'll be fine."

The trainer scoffed. "You can't pitch with that arm. Now let's go."

Where was...? No hope for Counsell going to bat for him now. Once Martin made the call, that was that. The manager had already returned to the dugout where Nolan's teammates looked on.

Nolan Ryan would have figured out a way to keep going. He was sure of it. The man had gotten in a fight on the mound, and now they sold autographed photographs of him with a busted lip and blood all over his shirt for upwards of five hundred bucks.

But he wasn't his namesake.

And to be fair, a split lip and a busted elbow were leagues apart when it came to pitching.

Nolan trudged down the mound to the sickening sound of cheers. The fans meant well, sure. Glad he could walk under his own power or some such. But the clapping grated as they celebrated the end of his opportunity to prove himself and get called up to the majors.

"How long?" He ground out the words as he forced his body forward.

Martin matched his pace toward the dugout. "Few weeks, probably. If it's not too bad, with care and therapy you might even be ready for the season."

The minor league season. This had been his shot. Without spring training, he'd never make the big-league roster. "Are they sending me back to Biloxi?"

They stepped down into the dugout where he avoided the guys' gazes. Would he find sympathy there? Or relief another man had been removed from the competition?

"That's not my call." Martin gestured him through the door.

In the medical area adjacent to the locker room, Nolan clenched his jaw and endured a series of prodding and poking, then a trip to the X-ray.

A half hour later, the team doctor narrowed his eyes at the picture. "Olecranon fracture. See this here?"

Nolan's stomach turned as the middle-aged doctor pointed to the black-and-white film. Even he knew his elbow bone shouldn't have a line going through it like that. "Surgery?"

The doctor clipped the image into a lighted display. "Fortunately, no. The bone is still intact and hasn't fragmented. You'll need immobility, rest, and physical therapy."

A little good news, at least. That sounded like a better play than going under the knife. "How long?"

"With this level of injury, most pitchers can return to the bullpen in about four months." The doctor leveled a look over his clipboard. "If they follow the treatment program."

Four months? His mouth dried. He'd go on the injured list, and they'd send him back to Biloxi where he'd have nothing to do for months but sit in his tiny apartment.

He could go back home three hours north of the Mississippi Coast to Brandon and stay with his folks. Dad would be disappointed. Probably tell him he should have done this, that, or the other to take better care of his arm. Dad would also encourage him, sure. But that wouldn't mask the disappointment. At twenty-six, Nolan was already two years past the age when Dad had been called up to the Braves.

"You got that?"

His attention snapped back to the doctor. "Sorry. What?"

"You'll be in the splint for four-to-six weeks. The doctor with the Shuckers will take periodic X-rays to check the healing. Ice as needed for swelling." The doctor scribbled something on his notepad. "Here's a prescription for the pain."

"I don't take anything stronger than Advil."

The doctor tore the page free and held it out to him. "Up to you. Have this filled if you change your mind."

Three hours later, Nolan plopped down on the hotel bed. The team had already secured tomorrow morning's ticket back to Mississippi. He fumbled his phone out of his pocket with his left hand and jabbed his finger against the screen.

He set it to speaker and settled against the headboard. Dad answered on the first ring. "What's the diagnosis?"

Of course, he already knew. He and Mom would have been watching the game on television. What had Dad done to stop Mom from calling before Nolan got back to the hotel?

"Olecranon stress fracture. Bone is still intact, so no surgery."

"Thank you, Lord." Mom's worried voice came through the speaker.

Dad remained silent.

"Six weeks in a sling. Then physical therapy. Doc says I should be able to start the regular season."

"But spring training is shot." Dad's matter-of-fact tone held little emotion. Another year gone. If Nolan didn't move up soon, he'd remain a career minor leaguer.

"Why don't you come stay with us?" Mom's sweet voice grated where she meant to soothe. "You'll need help without the use of your right arm."

Right. Getting on the plane was going to be trouble enough. "We'll see."

"Amelia's home."

Dad's two words had Nolan straightening. "What happened? Shouldn't she be working in Atlanta?"

"Came home three days ago. Something about her internship not working out."

"Actually," Mom supplied, "she and Sarah are going to Biloxi this weekend."

Despite all logic, his pulse quickened. The girl next door, his best friend's little sister, was off-limits. Didn't matter that his buddy had been gone for three years now. Derick would have punched him for making eyes at his sister.

The smile in Mom's voice revealed she knew what he'd worked hard to hide. "Sarah said they were going to take a mother-daughter trip to a B&B down there."

Dad chuckled. "I'm sure they'd love to see you, son."

Yeah. He might give her a call. "Maybe they'd like to have lunch while they're in town."

After another plea from Mom to come spend his recovery at home where she could smother him in motherly affection and a short conversation about Dad's experience with players who'd had similar injuries, Nolan said his goodbyes and disconnected.

Amelia Cabrera. Even if she wasn't his late best friend's sister, she was out of his league. That perfect honey-beige complexion and velvety-brown hair. He shook off the mental image of her charming smile.

He scrolled through his contacts and found the number for the Cabrera house, one of the few people he knew who still had a landline. He pressed the number and waited.

"*Hola*! Cabrera residence." Sarah's warm voice filled the line. To hear her now, you'd never know the blond-haired, blue-eyed woman hadn't spoken a word of Spanish until the birth of her first child. She'd done an incredible job of keeping her husband's Cuban heritage alive.

"Hola, Mrs. Cabrera. This is Nolan."

"How are you? Is baseball going well?"

He wiggled the fingers on his right hand and withheld a wince. "Small injury. I'm headed back to Biloxi tomorrow."

"What a shame. I'll pray for a swift recovery."

"Thank you." He cleared his throat. "Mom said you and Amelia would also be headed down to Biloxi? If so, we should all get together for lunch while y'all are in town."

"*Sí*!" She lowered her voice. "Amelia could use some time with a friend. I'll tell her you're coming. You two can have a good time without me."

That might not be the best—

"Oh. Here she is now."

Before he could respond, Amelia spoke. "Hello?"

"Hey." A pause. "This is Nolan." So lame.

"Hey. One sec. What Mamá?"

Nolan cringed. Sarah would make it sound like he'd asked her to lunch. Not both of them, which would be way less awkward.

"I talked to your mom about—"

"He did?" The surprised words cut off his explanation. "I'd love to have lunch with you, Nolan. It'll be great to catch up."

Was that a smile in her voice? "Yeah. Where are you staying? I'll pick you up." Oops. Driving would be a challenge with one arm. He could always call a rideshare.

"We'll be at The Depot in Ocean Springs. It's an old Victorian house they turned into a B&B. Saturday at twelve?"

"Sounds good."

"Then it's a date. See you then." The line went dead.

A date? Nolan stared at the phone. Did he have a *date* with Amelia?

A sensation wound through his chest he couldn't place. Maybe having to go back to Biloxi early wouldn't be so bad after all.

Three

Oh boy. They should have booked a room at the Best Western. Amelia mustered a smile as she gazed at the old house. The turrets and sweeping porches had a certain charm. But it probably didn't come with Wi-Fi. And the sign said something about stepping back in time—inn with two *N*s, not one. Quirky *and* old.

"It's *muy bonita*, yes?" Mamá extended her suitcase handle and clicked the button to lock her sedan. "Oh, look at that swing!"

"Very pretty, Mamá. Thank you for bringing me."

Mamá wrapped her in a hug. "Can you believe I was able to get us two rooms, with a full breakfast included, for seventy-five percent off? Something about a celebration weekend package."

Deep discounts could mean they were desperate for clients. Maybe for good reason. Mamá loved a good deal, though. Found them impossible to resist. "Yep. Great deal."

Amelia scoured the house's façade for signs of termites or whatever other critters an ancient house might hide but found nothing. The paint looked fresh, and every inch of the swept porch evidenced attentive care.

Mamá rang the doorbell. Another odd thing about not staying in a hotel. So weird to be renting a room in someone's house.

The door flew open, and a woman with gray curls and a beaming smile clapped her hands. "You're here! Right on time, no less. Not that I would expect anything different, mind you."

Amelia exchanged a glance with Mamá. What was this lady wearing?

Mamá didn't seem to notice. "Such a beautiful house!"

"Thank you, dear. Do come in." The exuberant woman arced the door to allow them entrance.

Amelia slid a subtle gaze over the woman as she passed. Was there a *Great Gatsby* costume party going on or something? The navy-blue dress featured fringes in layers from collarbone to calf and a matching beaded headband wrapped her temples. Weird. Normal people didn't dress like that on a regular Saturday. If this lady was nuts, it didn't bode well for their weekend.

But it might explain the deep discount.

They followed the woman over polished floors and past a grand staircase. "Over there is the kitchen and dining area, but Amelia doesn't need to go in there yet. It's not quite time."

What did she mean by that?

They entered a library where ceiling-high shelves should be sagging under the number of books shoved on them. Everything appeared antique, from the crystal lamps to the woven rug.

"Here we are. Rooms two and three." The woman in the funky costume held up two four-inch black metal keys.

Great. She'd have to take a purse just to keep up with that thing.

"Oh, heavens. Where are my manners? I'm Mrs. Easley, your hostess to history."

Mamá grinned, but Amelia had to withhold a grimace. Nothing stuffier than at bunch of history.

No, that wasn't fair. Her sour mood was all because she'd had to tuck tail and come home from Atlanta. A failure. Just thinking about the situation had her stomach fluttering the entire three-hour ride.

Not because she was nervous about seeing Nolan again. That would be ridiculous. And definitely not because she'd called their lunch today a date. He'd probably laughed after she'd panicked and hung up.

"Nice to meet you." Amelia forced cheer into her words. Mamá was doing something special for her, and she wasn't going to let her wayward emotions ruin it.

They followed the woman to the second floor and turned at the top of the stairs.

Mrs. Easley handed Mamá a key. "You are number two, right there. Why don't you go ahead and get settled? I've left a tray of cookies for you."

After Mamá tugged her suitcase over the thick carpet and twisted her key in the lock, Amelia held her hand out to Mrs. Easley for the key to the adjacent room.

The woman paused, proffering the ornate metal key. "Come down to the kitchen after you've unpacked. I have something to show you."

Right. Because that didn't sound creepy. "Um, I'll ask Mamá after we get settled."

"Just you, dear."

Yeah. That didn't make it weirder. Amelia ran her palm down her jeans. Maybe she should try to talk Mamá into the Best Western after all.

"You're a chef, right?" Mrs. Easley fiddled with a fringe on her dress. "I believe your mother mentioned it. This time of year, we get rather busy, and I was thinking of hiring a summer chef for parties and such."

Oh. Okay, so not quite as creepy. "I'll be heading back home soon, but thanks for thinking of me."

Mrs. Easley held out her key. "Ah, well, of course you'd have other plans. But maybe you can have a look at a recipe that's been giving me trouble? Tell me if I have something off on my measurements?"

"Uh, sure." Amelia plucked the key from the woman's fingers and scurried to her door.

It took three attempts before she got the old lock to work and shoved her way inside, closing the door on the crazy woman in the hall.

Her room met every expectation of a house intent on living in the past. No television. Just a giant wardrobe some curious kids could wander into and find themselves in a snowy fantasy realm, a petite writing desk, and a bed with a princess-style canopy. In rose pink, no less.

Amelia squished her fingers into the rose-and-green patchwork quilt. At least the mattress looked comfortable. She tossed her suitcase on the bed and, after a bit of searching, located a socket behind the desk. She plugged in her charger and phone and then tugged her long hair into a ponytail.

Her stomach rumbled. How come Mrs. Easley hadn't left *her* any cookies? No matter. She'd get one from Mamá and avoid the trip into the kitchen.

After a peek to make sure the proclaimed "hostess to history" didn't wait in the hall, Amelia ducked out of her room and tapped on the next door.

Mamá grinned as soon as she opened it. "My room is charming. How about yours?"

Amelia stepped into a similar version of her accommodations, except this one had been decorated in shades of blue. "It's cute." Her gaze landed on the tray on the dresser. "Mind if I grab one?"

"Help yourself." Mamá shook out a yellow sundress and looped the straps over the hanger. "They're your favorite."

Amelia lifted a white-chocolate-chip macadamia-nut cookie about the size of her palm from the painted plate and pinched off a piece. Great texture. Soft without crumbling. She popped the piece in her mouth and closed her eyes as the sweetness enveloped her palate.

Perfect balance of flavors with the right crunch from the nuts. Mrs. Easley had skills. Maybe it wouldn't hurt to check out that recipe for her. As long as Mamá came.

"I'm going to take a quick nap and then enjoy that garden while you go on your date with Nolan."

"It's not a date."

Mamá closed the wardrobe and set her empty suitcase next to it. Her cornflower gaze sparkled. "It's okay if it is, you know."

Was it though? They'd grown up together. Nolan and Derick, the cool older boys, and her, the nosy taga-long. He'd never see her as anything other than that cherub-faced little girl. She finished the cookie and debated snagging a second, but she'd promised herself she'd stop eating her feelings.

"Your Papá and Derick would both approve." Mamá handed her another cookie and nibbled her own. "Nolan is a good Christian man."

The thought of the missing half of their family squeezed the tender place that still hadn't healed. "I miss them."

"Me too, mijita." Mamá's warm arms settled around her waist, and Amelia absorbed her mother's comforting gardenia scent. Mamá pulled back to look in her eyes. "We will see them again in heaven. But for now, we must keep living, yes? We honor them the best we can."

The sentiment knifed through her core. Was she honoring her Papá by refusing to reopen his restaurant? The memories still simmered too close to the surface. Papá's hands guiding hers in making fresh tortillas even while making sure she knew they weren't traditionally Cuban. Derick teasing her when his arroz con leche turned out better than hers.

"Have a nice lunch, mijita. There's no pressure." Mamá pecked a kiss on Amelia's temple. "But go get ready and think about what I said. There's no harm in seeing where God and your heart leads. When you get back, I thought we'd do a little shopping before supper."

Amelia allowed Mamá to shoo her out the door and smothered a sigh. The only harm would be to her heart. Not something she planned on risking.

Even as she told herself several times this was *not* a date, she adjusted the straps on her green sundress and frowned at the mirror. Five fewer pounds and it would fit much better. Not that she could do anything about that now. She checked her watch. He'd be here soon. She should head downstairs. Maybe wait for him on the porch.

No. That looked too eager.

She'd reached the bottom step before she remembered the main reason she should have stayed in her room.

"Oh, good! There you are." Mrs. Easley's musical voice materialized beside her. "I'd begun to worry about the schedule. It was my understanding you were the type to be early, but no matter."

What did any of that mean? Amelia eyed the door. Would Mamá be mortified if she bolted and ignored the crazy woman trying to lure her into the kitchen?

The doorbell saved her from making that call.

Mrs. Easley bustled past in a swish of fringe with much more agility than she'd credit to an elderly person. The door swung wide, and Amelia's heart felt like it took a trip through Mamá's salad spinner.

Perfect dark curls. Strong jaw dusted in a hint of a beard. Wide shoulders that swung a bat and hurled a ball for a living. Chocolate eyes she could practically swim in. And...call her half-baked, but was he holding a fistful of yellow and red ruffled tulips? He smiled at Mrs. Easley, giving Amelia another few delicious seconds to stare.

Mamá said he'd had a minor injury, but Amelia hadn't expected his arm to be in a sling. What did that mean for his season?

She captured a fortifying breath and strode into the entry. Nolan's gaze snagged on her, and her pulse did a rumba through her veins when what seemed like admiration lit those cocoa-brown depths.

Get a grip. This was Nolan. He thought of her like a little sister. *Don't be weird.*

Right. Like she'd ever accomplished that feat.

She reached the door and stuck out her hand. "Nolan. Good to see you."

He blinked at her outstretched fingers, then shifted the flowers to pin them between his body and the arm in the sling.

So much for not being weird. Ugh. She dropped her hand. But that was worse, so she jerked it up again. Just in time to smack his away.

Heat raced into her cheeks. "Sorry."

Mrs. Easley tittered a musical laugh. "Come into the kitchen to get some water for those lovely blooms. And you two can have a sip of my lemonade before you go."

"Oh no, that's not—"

"Sure, we'd love to." Nolan cocked an eyebrow.

Right. The flowers. Should she take them from him or...?

He lifted them toward her. "These still your favorites?"

Why had her mouth gone dry? "Yep."

And now her voice squeaked. Perfect. Just perfect. She plucked them from his hold and forced herself to enact the professionalism she used in the kitchen. Well, right up until her last day, but now wasn't the time to dwell on that fiasco. "They are beautiful. Thank you."

She turned on her heel before he could laugh at what had to be the salsa-red condition of her face. Honestly. What was wrong with her?

They found Mrs. Easley in the kitchen filling a glass vase. She put the container on the counter. "Here you are, dear. A vessel to better display the perfection of the blooms."

She patted her hip like she was looking for something, though that dress couldn't possibly have any pockets.

Nolan slid onto a stool at the raised counter with the easy confidence that had always clung to him. Amelia took a second to admire the kitchen and give her pulse time to get itself under control.

The house might be outdated, but the kitchen was not. A gleaming Viking cooktop boasted six gas burners, and Mrs. Easley had two wall ovens positioned across from the double fridge. A substantial farmhouse sink rounded out the blend of old and new. Not bad.

"We've had a recent renovation." Mrs. Easley handed her a glass of sunny liquid. "Do you like it?"

"Very nice." Amelia took a sip. "Well, we should be going."

"Not yet, dear." Mrs. Easley pursed her lips and pulled them to one side. "Let's see. What was it Mr. Reed needed?" She snapped her fingers. "I remember."

When had they given her Nolan's name? She cut him a look, but the humor in the upturn of his brows said he didn't share her concern over the woman's weirdness.

Mrs. Easley fished something from a drawer. "Here we are. I believe you're familiar with George Herman, right?"

"George—you mean Babe Ruth?" Nolan reached for the card with all the gentleness of a new sous chef with a sea urchin.

Mrs. Easley let it fall to the counter before he could touch it and plucked something else from behind her. "And for you, my dear. Isn't it darling?" She held out an antique mixer. The kind with a crank handle that twisted the two whisks together.

The utensil was hardly on par with a mint-condition card of the Great Bambino, but okay. She took the tool with a weak smile. The red paint on the wooden handle had started to fade. "Sure."

Mrs. Easley stepped back and clasped her hands in front of her like she was waiting for something to happen.

As Nolan gingerly lifted the card from the counter, Amelia's vision grew fuzzy. She blinked, but the haze wouldn't go away.

Voices sounded like they were coming from far off, growing steadily closer. Tantalizing smells filled her nostrils, and the familiar sounds of a busy commercial kitchen assaulted her ears.

What was happening?

She swayed as the floor seemed to drop beneath her. Then everything went silent.

Four

"Excuse me, sir?" The masculine voice prodded Nolan's ear and attempted to tug him from a deep sleep.

He grunted and twisted on a stiff surface. Hard points poked into his back, but he couldn't seem to get his eyes to open. Oh well. Sleep was good.

"Sir? We need you to get up."

Nolan mentally swatted the buzzing voice. Had he fallen asleep in the dugout? No, that couldn't be right. He'd flown back to Biloxi. Then went to visit Amelia for their date.

Wait. Had they gone out? He couldn't remember. Forcing his mind to focus, he cracked one eyelid.

A portly man with a weird flat little cap frowned at him. "Sir. Guests will be arriving soon. If you hope to have employment here, you'll need to rouse yourself this instant."

Employment? What in the world was this guy rambling about? Nolan pried open his other eye and regarded the man in a red uniform.

He tugged on the hem of his brass-buttoned jacket. "Very good. Now, up you go. We'll get some coffee in you to sober you up, and I'll show you your duties."

Sober...? "I'm not drunk." Nolan sat up straighter, every muscle in his back complaining.

What in the world? Beyond the place where he sat on the unforgiving concrete, palm trees erupted from manicured grounds dotted with sprouting fountains. A curved drive held two shiny antique cars. A salty breeze washed over his face, carrying with it the familiar ocean scents.

This fancy place wasn't where Amelia and her mom were staying.

He pushed his palms to the ground and sprang to his feet. "Where am I?"

Ouch. He pressed his fingers to his temple as a wave of dizziness unsettled his balance. Why did he feel as though he was trying to shake off a coma?

"As I said." The man clasped his hands behind his back and leveled Nolan with a flat look. "We will sober you up first, then go over the specifics." He snapped his fingers. "This way please, Mr. Reed."

"How do you know my name?"

The man shuffled toward a set of carved doors. Another guy in the same suit held one open for them to pass through.

Crisp morning light filtered through a wall of windows and illuminated a high-end hotel lobby. Most definitely not the homey inn where he'd gone to pick up Amelia. Cold sweat prickled his skin.

Had he fallen and hit his head? He shoved his fingers into his hair, only to dislodge a striped cap that plopped onto the carpeted floor. He scooped up the cap and paused. Wait. He wiggled the fingers on his right hand. No pain. No sling.

"Mr. Reed? Really, we must be going." The red-faced man puffed out his cheeks and glanced around the empty room.

Nolan's gaze traveled from the white-and-blue striped old-style ball cap in his hand to the arched ceiling overhead. He let out a low whistle. "Fancy place. Where are we?"

The man pinched the bridge of his nose. "Bring in the ballplayers, he said. They can work here, he said." He snorted, rattling wide nostrils. "If you have any hope of keeping your position on Mr. Flagler's team, I suggest you make good on your duties."

Who? Nolan focused on the man again but couldn't make sense of his words. "My arm doesn't hurt."

"Well and good, seeing as how you are to pitch. Now, the coffee?"

Might as well go with it until he could clear his head and gather more information. He resumed his traipse through what had to be a fancy hotel lobby. High desks lined either side of the arched hallway, each with a friendly-looking man or woman waiting behind it. Dainty chandeliers dropped down at even intervals, creating patterns of light across the clusters of chairs or tables topped with flower arrangements and highlighted the carpet's floral motif.

Weird. Why was he wearing these funky leather shoes? He paused. And knee-high socks. Wait. When had he put on a baseball uniform? Especially one like this? Was it vintage night at the park or something?

His brain struggled to swim through the fog surrounding every thought. Man. This had to be the strangest dream he'd ever had. He should get that coffee the disgruntled fellow waving him forward offered.

He hadn't taken any of that pain medicine from the doc, had he? That might explain this dream. Or hallucination.

Whatever. But no, he only took ibuprofen. Uncle Jim had struggled for years with an addiction to prescription pills after a back injury. Nolan never took the stuff if he could manage.

They passed through a doorway and into a starkly different space. A flat ceiling replaced the soaring arches. Unadorned walls and those goofy-looking Edison lights some people used when they wanted to look vintage led the way to a room housing chairs and a table with a three-foot-tall silver jug.

It had a different name. But he had no idea what you called those big containers hotels used to hold gallons of coffee. Like a water cooler. But a coffee warmer.

Nolan paused in the doorway and shook his head. What was wrong with him? If he didn't know for certain he never drank alcohol, he might wonder if the man had been right about him needing to sober up.

"Hey, what's your name?"

The man finished filling a white ceramic mug and handed it to Nolan. "Presley Monroe. It's my duty to manage the baseball players and see that they have gainful employment while in Palm Beach."

Nolan blew the steam from the mug. "Did you say Palm Beach?"

Presley's jowls quivered. Weird. How'd he do that?

"Mr. Reed, you were scheduled to arrive on the train with the rest of the new boys last night. Apparently, while the others found their accommodations, you sir, decided to sleep by the front door. It's to your benefit I found you before any guests could notice you."

Okay. That answer didn't help at all. They must have the wrong Mr. Reed. He pulled the bitter liquid into his mouth and let it settle on his tongue before swallowing. "So, I'm supposed to work a job and play baseball?"

The man's already rosy complexion deepened to a brighter crimson. "Do you wish to be unemployed?"

"Baseball is my employment."

Presley scoffed. "Paid to play baseball? Who do you think you are? A Yankee?"

The coffee worked though his veins, and Nolan drew another sip to clear his brain. "Nope. Brewer."

"What?"

Nolan held the man's stare. "I'm a Brewer. Play AA for the franchise."

"That so?" Presley rocked back on his heels and jammed his fingers into his jacket pockets. "Don't know what any of that means, but I'm not the biggest baseball fan. All I know is that the Yankees and that new sensation, the man they call Babe, are going to play the Reds on St. Patrick's Day and now I'm inundated with boys who can't keep their heads out of the clouds. Supposed to employ them so the guests can watch the hotel teams from the Breakers and the Royal Poinciana square off."

Nolan's brain worked through the stream of words, catching on an unfamiliar phrase. Had he called Babe Ruth a new sensation? "Did you say Babe? As in Babe Ruth?"

Presley snagged a mug from the table and filled it halfway before turning back to Nolan. "You haven't heard? They bought his contract from the Red Sox in January."

In January? More like a hundred years ago. Maybe he should drink more coffee. Despite the heat, he drained the rest of the cup.

"Very good." Presley plunked his cup on the table and brushed his hands together. "Now, let's get you fitted for your uniform."

"Oh, I don't work here."

"If you want to play, you have to work. That's how Adams wants it."

"Who's Adams?"

Presley's lips pinched tight. "Your manager."

"Look, I don't know who you think I am. But I'm Nolan Reed, and I play for the Biloxi Shuckers. At least until I get called up."

Whatever the man's flapping jowls were working to say was cut off when the door opened. A man about Nolan's age stuck his head in, wheat-colored hair slicked back with way too much gel. His gaze landed on Nolan, and he brightened.

"You must be our new pitcher. Reed, right?"

Nolan cupped the back of his neck. Now that the coffee had taken effect and his mind had started to clear, a knot of ice took up residence in his stomach.

"Can you tell me where I am?"

The guy sauntered into the room, dressed in the same stuffy uniform as Presley. "You're at the Breakers. We play the Royal Poinciana for the guests. Good crowds too. Adams is working on getting a spring training program going here like what they got down in Miami. That's why the Reds and the Yankees are coming. He got them to stop here on the seventeenth after they play their two games down there. I heard that—"

"Mr. Olsen! Don't you have work to be about?" Presley's sour words fired through the air and made the younger man's mouth snap shut.

"Yes, Mr. Monroe. Except I was supposed to find all the new players." He thumbed toward Nolan. "Mr. Reed here's the last we're missing."

"Look." Nolan held up his hands. No pain in his elbow. Weird. But proof none of this was real. Right? "I don't know what's going on here, but I don't work for a hotel. I'm not a bellhop."

"You can be a waiter instead. Some of the guys are."

The look Presley shot—what had he called this excitable guy? Right, Mr. Olsen—had Mr. Olsen's lips scrunching as his gaze darted between the two of them.

"Are you in charge of the employees now, Mr. Olsen? Should I inform Mr. McGinnis? Or perhaps we should go straight to Mr. Flagler and tell him the men *he* hired are no longer needed, as you are clearly capable of assigning employment."

The color drained from Olsen's face, only to be replaced by enough blood to match his uniform. "Sorry, sir."

Poor guy. He looked like a little leaguer about to try to pitch to Mark McGwire.

Nolan patted Presley on the back, which earned a sputter. "I'll go with Olsen here and get all this straightened out, yeah?"

Before Presley could object, Nolan followed Olsen into the hallway.

As soon as the door clicked behind them, Olsen nudged Nolan's side. "Let's skedaddle. We'll get you out to the field and put off hauling luggage for the rich folks awhile longer. I'm Pete, by the way. You can call me Pete. I heard you were a right good pitcher. Strong arm. Where'd you play before? Me, I came right out of the cornfields in Nebraska. My pa said I wouldn't ever make it to play ball, but I'm proving him wrong. This is a good start. You'll see."

More words poured from Pete's mouth as they hurried down the hallway, but Nolan couldn't focus on any of them.

The last thing he remembered was going to the B&B to meet Amelia. They'd been in the kitchen, and he'd picked up a mint-condition Ruth card that had to be worth at least as much as a Derek Jeter salary. Then...what?

He'd felt a little dizzy. Amelia had put her hands over her ears and started to sway.

Nolan stopped short.

Oh no. What had happened to Amelia?

Five

S he needed a second to close her eyes. Amelia sucked in a breath to clear the sudden headache. She could have sworn she heard voices that had *not* been in the kitchen with her. The stress must be getting to her. Nolan, her job...

Oh right. Better get herself together before he thought she'd lost it. Smile in place.

Her eyelids popped open, and a yelp tore through her throat.

She gripped a wooden tabletop to keep from falling over. Gone was the cute little kitchen in a Victorian seaside inn. She blinked, but the vision before her refused to budge. Had she been teleported to something from one of her history lessons?

A twenty-foot-long cast-iron, coal-burning range and a broiler with a mechanical spit dominated one wall. A shiny metalwork island manned in the center of the room topped with marble and a pedestal large enough to grind an entire turkey.

Light filtered through a dozen windows, illuminating an expanse of open shelving hosting pots, pans, and utensils of every shape, size, and make.

Where...where *was* she?

At voices behind her, Amelia whirled as two women, one in her fifties and the other probably still in high school, entered through a solid wooden door. They stopped when their gazes landed on her.

The older of the two, a short woman with gray streaks in her coffee-colored bun and strong Latina features cocked an eyebrow. "Señorita, you are *muy* early, sí?"

Very early for what?

The woman waved her hand. "No matter. It is good. Shows you are ready to work."

What?

The younger fair-haired woman scurried to a wall of aprons and plucked one from the hook.

"I am Señora Cabrera." The older woman flicked an apron around her waist. "Why are you holding that mixer?"

44

What? Oh. The mixer she'd taken from Mrs. Easley still nestled in her palm. But wait. Did that mean...?

The red-handled contraption clattered to the brick floor like it'd caught fire.

The older woman arched a brow. "*¿Estás bien?* Are you all right, miss...?"

"Amelia. I'm Amelia—" Wait. What had this woman said her name was? "Cabrera."

The heavy metal door on the wall-sized oven banged. The blond stretched red lips over perfect teeth. "That's Tita's name too. You two related?"

Now that she mentioned it, Señora Cabrera did bear a remarkable resemblance to pictures of Papá's grandmother. But that was ridiculous. Her *bisabuela* died when Amelia was only seven.

Señora Cabrera—Tita—rolled her eyes. "Is every person with the name Smith related?"

The girl's cheeks colored, but her smile never wavered. "I suppose not. Though it's a funny coincidence, I say."

Tita waved a dish towel at her. "Get on with you. There's work to do." She focused on Amelia. "You too. We will get started. Aprons are over there."

"I'm not supposed to be here." The words stuck to the roof of her mouth like peanut butter, but she forced them out anyway.

"Then where are you supposed to be?"

"On a date with Nolan." Those slippery words popped free of their own accord before she could hold them back.

The girl gathering pots from the wall giggled.

"Hush, Edna." Tita nestled a hand on her rounded hip. "Date?" She blew out a heavy breath. "You *chicas* and your modern ideas. Get to work. We have too much to do for woolgathering."

Um... Amelia accepted the apron handed to her. "I don't think you understand. I was in a different kitchen a couple of minutes ago, about to go on a date with this guy who I've always secretly had a thing for, and then"—she snapped her fingers—"poof! I'm here. It's totally crazy, I know, but that's what happened."

Tita shooed her toward the sink. "You're not one of those chicas thinking she's going to be in pictures, are you?"

Pictures?

"Fill three pots and get them on the stove."

The woman spoke with such authority that Amelia found her hands following through with the task despite the panic attempting to boil over in her stomach.

She needed to think. That was all. She'd been in the kitchen with Nolan and Mrs. Easley. The older woman had handed her the mixer, and then...she'd ended up here.

That was it!

The copper pot clanged in the bottom of the cast-iron sink, and Amelia bolted across the room. Tita shouted, and Edna yipped like a startled puppy. Amelia snatched the mixer up from the counter where Tita must have placed it and held it up in the air.

Nothing happened.

Grinding her teeth, she grabbed the handle and cranked the whisks. Still nothing. But this had to be it. This *had* to be what had teleported her to, well, wherever she was. Tears burned in the back of her eyes and slid down her cheeks like molten chocolate.

She'd lost her mind. The stress from the failure in Atlanta had made her crack. And...and...

A warm hand rested on her shoulder, and gentle fingers plucked the mixer from her grasp. Tita wrapped her in an embrace. She smelled like home. Like fresh cilantro and Abuela's hand cream.

Sobs wrenched from Amelia's throat, and she let the fear leak out of her all over Tita's brown polka-dotted dress.

"There now, *pequeña*. What troubles you?"

Papá had also called her "little one." "Papá. I miss him and my brother. They are gone. And now I'm here and...Mamá. She must be terrified."

Tita stroked her back. "All is well. We will pray, sí?"

47

She eased Amelia away to look into her face and offered a sympathetic smile. Then a heartfelt and beautiful prayer flowed in perfect Spanish from her lips and glided like fresh butter over Amelia's battered emotions.

Tita finished and patted her shoulder. "You might not have understood, but God does."

"I speak Spanish." Amelia wiped her eyes. "My father was Cuban."

"Oh? I am also *Cubana*."

"See?" Edna piped up from where she dumped coffee grounds into a kettle. "You could be related."

Tita rolled her eyes again and produced an actual handkerchief from her pocket to hand to Amelia. "We thought you were the new young cook come to help us. Are you not her?"

"Help where? I don't even know where we are."

"Hey! Señora!" A male voice called from the doorway. He pronounced "señora" like a drawn-out "sin-your-uh."

A second later, a guy in a red uniform and slicked-back hair entered the room with a taller man close on his heels.

Her stomach dove for her toes.

"Nolan!"

Nolan's heart dropped like Jordan Hick's sinker. Then it took a line drive to his throat. "Amelia! What are you doing here?"

He trotted into a cavernous kitchen and snagged the last person he thought he'd see here into a hug. But then, if this was a hallucination brought on by pain meds, maybe it did make sense. She buried her face into his chest, and he held her tight. Yeah. Totally a hallucination. The real Amelia never let her emotions show. And she never needed anyone to coddle her. Especially not him.

The hallucination adjusted to his thoughts, and she shoved away from him. "Where are we? Do you know what's going on?"

He looked at Pete, who had made a beeline for the perky blond over by a stove clunky enough to be a train engine. No wonder the guy had wanted this pit stop by the kitchen before they went to the field. Clearly, it hadn't actually been for getting oranges.

Focusing on the owllike eyes of the woman in front of him, Nolan smoothed his hands down her shoulders. Hallucination Amelia wouldn't mind. She wore a pink dress with a low waist that looked pretty on her. Of course, most things looked pretty on her.

Her lips parted as she looked up at him, the swarm of emotions swirling in them too complicated for his mind to have generated. Maybe this wasn't a figment of his imagination.

If that was the case, then he needed to get it together. Act cool and in control.

"Thought you might know." Stupid. Why'd he go and say that?

"Why would I know?" She pursed her lips and cut a glance at an older woman rolling dough on a metal table before she shrugged off his touch and glowered at his uniform. "And why are you dressed in a vintage uniform?"

Because nothing happening today made any sense. "I'm supposed to play baseball when I'm not working as a bellhop."

"What?" Her nose wrinkled. "Why are you a bellhop?"

"Why are you working in a hotel kitchen?"

The woman behind them muttered something in Spanish he didn't quite catch, but he ignored her.

"What hotel?" Amelia rubbed her temples. "You're not making any sense."

He tucked his hand behind her waist and guided her to a corner wall crammed with pots and pans. He ducked his head close to hers and lowered his voice. "I woke up sitting outside of what I was told is the Breakers Hotel." He hesitated. "In Palm Beach."

"What!"

Her screech had the older woman glaring at him, hands firm on her rounded hips.

"Shhh." He cast the woman an apologetic look and turned his back to her, hiding Amelia behind his larger frame. "You asked. I'm telling. You want this story or not?"

She tugged on a strand of hair like she always did when she got stressed but didn't want anyone to know. "That doesn't make sense. We went to Biloxi. That's like—What? Twelve hours away?"

Yeah. He didn't say he understood it. "All I know is I woke up here, wearing this. People knew my name. Expected me to be here." He fiddled with a seam on his pants. This next part would be worse, and she was already looking pretty pale. "It gets weirder."

She crossed her arms. "I highly doubt that."

"There's lots of talk going around about a game on St. Patrick's Day. Turns out, there's a baseball field here, between two of these rich-people hotels."

"So?"

Did she know how cute she looked when she lowered her chin like that and tried to give him a stern look?

Nolan rubbed the back of his neck. "Well, the weird part is they keep saying Babe Ruth will be there."

She stared at him, her eyes as blank as the locker room's freshly painted walls.

"Babe Ruth. As in the real Babe Ruth."

A spark fired in those velvet-brown depths. "Nolan. That man died like, a hundred years ago."

"In 1948, actually."

She threw out her hands. "Do you hear yourself?"

The woman rolling dough said something else in Spanish he was pretty sure compared him to a scarecrow with nothing more than straw for brains.

He started to shove his hands in his pockets. But the uniform didn't have any, so he awkwardly crossed his arms. "Remember how we were in the B&B's kitchen?"

She glared at him.

Right. Duh. "I picked up that Babe Ruth card, remember? And you picked up that old mixer. I started to feel dizzy, and you looked like you didn't feel well either. Next thing I know, we're here."

"How does that explain anything?"

He had a hunch, but it sounded more far-fetched than his chances of winning the Cy Young award this year. He held up his right hand and flexed his fingers. "Remember how I fractured my elbow? And I'm supposed to be out for the next few weeks?"

Shiny brown eyes widening, she grabbed his hand and inspected his fingers. "What happened? Is it better?"

"Shouldn't be."

Her thumb made a circular pattern over his knuckles as she studied him. Weird how such a mundane touch fired through his nerves. Not that he was complaining.

"Señorita." The older woman blew out a breath. "The time for working is now. The time for what you call 'dating,' this is for after work, sí?"

Heat rocketed up his neck. Had Amelia said something to this woman about them dating?

Across the room, Pete smirked. Great.

"One moment, Señora Cabrera." Amelia transformed into the perfectly-put-together woman he recognized. Her posture straightened, and all traces of panic disappeared from her voice. "This is my friend. We've found ourselves in a somewhat strange situation."

The woman muttered something else under her breath and went back to her dough with more force than necessary.

Amelia clenched his arm with surprising strength and huddled him further into the corner. "I don't understand anything you're talking about." She pushed words through clenched teeth. "Your arm doesn't hurt, and that's great. But what does that have to do with Palm Beach and Babe Ruth?"

He swallowed a glob in his throat. "Call me crazy, but I think, um, well—"

"Oh, just spit it out!"

"I think we went back in time. Like the sign said." He blurted out the stupidest thing he'd ever uttered. Best explanation he'd come up with, though. It *had* been right there in plain writing. "Step back 'inn' *time* and leave your troubles behind."

"You've got to be kidding me." Amelia stepped away from him, eyes going wild. She closed her lids over the simmering fire. "That's not possible. I got dizzy. Fell and hit my head. Right now, I'm in a coma at the hospital dreaming up some weird story. And Nolan is here, of course, because I let my stupid heart think we were going on a date. I was stressed about it. Yep. That's it. Now I need to wake up."

Um... Should he give her a moment or figure out something to say to that?

Her eyelids popped open, and her shoulders slumped.

He stretched his lips into a smile he hoped was both convincing and charming. "It's okay. You're not in a coma. I'm really here with you, promise."

The professional chef returned. Gordon Ramsey spine of steel. "We need to fix this. Right now."

Did that mean she believed him?

"Do we?" The question slipped between his lips, tasting oddly sweet. "I mean, it's cool, right? Think about it. We can see the 1920 Yankees. See Babe Ruth play."

"Are you hearing yourself? You've lost your mind." Amelia took a step back from him and bumped into the shelving, dislodging a copper kettle that clattered to the brick floor.

The woman who had been muttering Spanish while rolling dough and periodically casting him heated looks slammed down her rolling pin and stalked in their direction. "Enough! *Jovencito*, I think it is time you go to your job. Out of my kitchen."

"I'm sorry, Mrs.—" Nolan held up his hands. "Wait. Did you say her name is Cabrera?"

Amelia pinched her lips together.

"That is my name, yes." Mrs. Cabrera snorted. "Now, out."

Pete sidled up next to the aproned woman. "Best we skedaddle. Adams will be waiting on us anyway." He grinned at the older woman. "Thanks for letting us stop by. Got anything you want me to take to the mister?"

Her eyes softened as she patted him on the cheek. "You are a good boy. But no, not today. I am already too far behind."

Nolan leaned close to Amelia, and the scent of her plumeria body spray—the same kind she'd worn since the ninth grade—swarmed his senses. He shoved as many words into this final moment as he could.

"This is 1920. She has your name. What if you got sent back in time so you could meet her? A great-great-grandmother who is also a chef? Think about it. Isn't she the one who wrote that recipe book you always try to cook from but can't ever get anything right?"

Her lips parted. No words came free.

Before he could think better of it, he tugged her to him, kissed her forehead, and jogged after Pete.

Six

This was crazy. Amelia whipped her emotions into submission and smeared a smile in place as Nolan sauntered out of the kitchen. Only a figment of her own making would fling a handful of ghost peppers into her ice cream and stride off as though he hadn't ruined dessert.

Time traveling. Ridiculous!

And kissing her? On the forehead, yeah. Like a brother might, sure. But it hadn't *felt* like what a brother would do. At least not to her. And he walked away like nothing had happened.

"Señora Cabrera?" When the woman met her gaze over the island, Amelia forced stupid words out of her mouth. "What year is it?"

"Simple Tita is fine." Her hands worked the fine dough, pulling, rolling, and stretching. "Are you going to start working, or do I need to send you on your way?"

Right. No work, no answers. Amelia grabbed a white cotton apron, secured it around her waist, then took a place beside Tita, and waited for instruction.

A stream of women entered before she could repeat the ridiculous question she wanted answered. Ten of them in total, ranging from as young as Edna to possibly twice the middling years of Tita. With cheerful conversations and quick hands, they flowed into the easy rhythm of people accustomed to commercial kitchens. A couple gave her a friendly nod, but most went about their morning.

"Why do you ask such a strange question?" Tita pinched the edge of the dough, then wiped her hands down her apron. Her probing gaze held only curiosity.

A nervous laugh bubbled up Amelia's throat. "Nolan said this is 1920. Isn't that crazy?"

"*Loco*? Why?"

Not good. She forced calm into her voice. "Oh, nothing."

This was a dream. So of course, it could be whatever year her mind wanted it to be. Didn't feel like a fantasy though. Not with the swarm of smells and the clatter of pots. But time traveling? To Florida? Ridiculous.

Nolan's words refused to stop making a loop through her brain. *What if you got sent back in time so you could meet her? A great-great-grandmother who is also a chef?*

"You wouldn't happen to have an old family recipe book, would you?" Amelia fiddled with the edge of her apron. "One with traditional recipes from the Cabrera family?"

A dark eyebrow arched. "How would you know this? Did my Rico tell you?" She blew a breath up her face. Something over Amelia's shoulder snagged her attention, and she waved a hand. "Mary! Not so many onions!"

The brunette ducked her head and placed the rest of the chopping board covered in diced onions on the counter.

"That man. Always with the pranks." Tita skirted around the island and bustled toward the stove, leaving no option except to follow. She motioned for another girl to take over the dough and gave rapid-fire instructions to two others before focusing back on Amelia. "Do you have any experience?"

With pranks? She stared at the woman. Oh. Right. Kitchen work. She must look nuts. "I completed culinary school in New Orleans and interned in Atlanta." A pang shot through her stomach. No reason to give more details on that disaster unless she had to.

"You have worked outside of a home kitchen before?"

"My entire life. My father owned a restaurant."

Tita's flour-dusted hand flew to her throat. "Then why are you here and not..." Whatever expression marred Amelia's face made Tita's words drizzle to a stop. "No. *Perdóname.* This is not my business." She smacked her hands together. "Come. You will make the ensalada."

Salad? Really? How much more basic could her assignment get? Boiling water? But she had to wake up eventually. Maybe her mind just needed her to do a little mental therapy of sorts. Go through the motions of culinary work. See Nolan. Confess her crush.

Wait. No. Where had *that* thought come from? Now who was *loca*?

With nothing else to do, she busied her hands chopping lettuce and dicing red onions. Soon, her shoulders inched down from her ears. This was what she needed. A simple task surrounded by the delectable scents of a kitchen in full swing.

"Good." Tita's voice startled her from tossing the cherry tomatoes into the sink-sized salad bowl. "You can work a knife, at least. Now, take this basket and get out to the garden. Rico will send you back with the herbs."

Fresh herbs? Lovely. She cleaned her hands on a towel and looped the woven basket over her elbow. "Where's the garden?"

Simple instructions led her through a back door, down a short hall, and out into a world of sunshine. A low brick wall surrounded an inviting space brimming with fragrant herbs, hearty vegetables, and an abundance of birdsong. She paused and savored a long breath. A warm breeze seasoned with the ocean caressed her cheeks.

"You've come for the señora's spices, no?" The heavily accented male voice sounded from behind her, and she almost dropped the basket.

"Hello. Yes."

Dressed in typical gardener attire, complete with floppy sun hat and work-worn boots, the middle-aged man leaned on a rake and regarded her with tented brows. "You came from the kitchen?"

Something in his tone stirred her defenses. "I did."

"You want to be a cook?"

Why did he sound so incredulous? She plopped a hand on her hip. "I'm a professional chef."

"You?" A laugh burst from his linen-clad chest. "No. Cannot be."

"Excuse me?" How dare he stand there laughing at her? She pinned him with a glare she hoped was as sharp as one of Papá's knives. "And why not? Because I'm a woman?"

Twinkling brown eyes slid behind half-lowered lids. "No, not that. Best cooks in the world are always women. Ask any *mujer*, and she will tell you."

Of all the nerve! She didn't care one grain of rice what this old man thought. "Then why?"

"Too skinny."

The anger dissipated like a water droplet on a hot griddle. "What?"

"Sí. A woman who loves her food is not afraid to taste it." He pushed off the rake and propped the tool against a tree. "Like *mi amor*. She is perfect in every way, yes? No fear of tasting for her."

Never in her life had she been both insulted and complimented by the same statement. Too skinny to be a chef. Who ever heard of such a thing?

The strange man plodded to a low table shielded by a fragrant orange tree and picked up a bundle of cut herbs. He held them out to her, but when she reached for them, he pulled back. "What have you brought for me?"

"I don't have anything for you."

His dirt-crusted hand landed over his heart with a thud. "Oh! *Mi corazón.* She sends me nothing?"

"Tita?"

"Who else but the light of my life, the sunshine of my world?"

Oh boy. What a character. Still, a smile sneaked over her lips despite herself. "Sorry. She didn't send anything."

He clucked his tongue and placed the bundles of basil, cilantro, dill, and rosemary into her basket as gently as a mother with a newborn.

"Thanks. I'll take these to the kitchen."

"Sí, sí. And give my love to my sunshine, even though she did not send her pastelitos to ease the ache in my stomach. And my heart."

This time she couldn't help laughing. Such drama over a pastry. "I will tell her."

He waved to her as she ambled through the garden, reluctant to return inside. What must it be like to still be so silly in love at that age? Had they been married long? Or was it a new thing?

She found Tita watching over the shoulder of a mousy woman sautéing onions with every ounce of the intimidation of Chef Dubois. As soon as Tita spotted her, she moved away, and the poor girl's shoulders drooped.

Tita rifled through the basket. "Good. We'll put these in the icebox."

"The gardener sends his love."

Tita's full lips twitched into a smile. "Even without his treat? He must be in a fine mood today."

She could say that. "How long have you two been married?"

Amelia followed Tita through the busy line of sous chefs and to a humming head-high white cabinet. Tita lifted a metal handle to open the antique version of a refrigerator and began placing the cut ends of the herbs into waiting water tubs.

"Since we were seventeen. We came to this country together with nothing more than our love and the clothes we wore."

The moisture evaporated from Amelia's mouth like her body had turned into a two-thousand-degree oven. She'd heard that story before. Of how her ancestors had come from Cuba. Two newlyweds with nothing but a dream.

She forced her tongue to form words. "And children?"

"Sí."

Three boys.

"We had three sons."

Luis, Carlo...

"Carlo, Luis, and—"

Amelia's throat seized, and she fired out the name pounding through her heart. "Manuel."

Tita withdrew from the fridge and narrowed her eyes. "Did Rico tell you already?"

Her pulse thudded in her ears. Papá's great-grandfather. His namesake. The youngest son born to the brave couple who had been the first of their family to move to America. "You're...you're Martita and Federico Cabrera."

Tita and Rico for short.

Tita settled a hand on Amelia's back, her fingers warm. Deep-brown eyes held hers. "Do you need to sit down? You're looking pale."

She couldn't make her mouth answer or her body move.

Could Nolan be right? Had she traveled back in time to meet her third great-grandmother?

Her stomach lurched, and an infuriating bout of nausea attempted to march up her throat.

Seven

The smell of fresh-cut grass mingled with briny air put a bounce in Nolan's step as they hurried from the rear of the Breakers Hotel and toward an open swath of land that would surely be packed with development in his own time. He and Pete neared a baseball field where roofs sporting triangle banners topped wooden bleachers. The diamond stood between the opulent structure behind them and another impressive hotel. That had to be the Royal Poinciana, the other Flagler hotel everyone had talked about. Seemed the two hotel teams played regular games for the guests. Though he hadn't figured out if they were bellhops with baseball positions or ballplayers who moved luggage on the side.

The distinction mattered.

"Not bad, eh?" Pete nudged Nolan with a bony elbow. "Nothing fancy like they got in Brooklyn or Boston, but I'll take the weather here any day."

"Maybe not in August."

Pete snorted. "They all go back north once summer sets in good. This here is a winter-and-spring sort of operation."

The familiar smack of a ball striking into the pitcher's mitt eased the tension in Nolan's center. Men practiced drills in the infield, though this didn't appear to be a formal exercise.

They passed through a wooden gate near the first baseline stands and then through another to gain entrance to the dirt infield. Funny how baseball hadn't changed in a hundred years. Sure, the bags looked lumpy and the chalk lines weren't as clear, and he was pretty sure once he found a ball he'd really spot the differences, but home plate and the mound remained constant.

A man could feel at home on any field. No matter where—or in this case *when*—it might be. And in a few days, Babe Ruth and the 1920s New York Yankees would play on this very spot. Too bad he didn't have that card from Mrs. Easley. He could have gotten an autograph.

The six guys in the field noticed them approaching and offered friendly waves. He returned the gesture, energy bubbling through him. Babe Ruth would play right here. And Bob Shawkey or Carl Mays might stand on that very mound.

Nolan flexed the fingers on the arm that should be in a sling. No pain. "Mind if I throw a few?"

Pete's thin shoulders hitched toward his oversized ears. "Reckon you can if you want. But better not stay too long and get old Monroe's knickers in a wad. He's strict about making sure we are still doin' our jobs."

"Sure. I understand."

One fellow in his midtwenties tucked a catcher's mitt under his arm and jogged over. He pushed a long-brimmed blue hat up his forehead. "You that new pitcher?"

Was he? "Guess so."

"You sure are a big fella." The guy grinned and spat a stream of tobacco juice. "Let's see what you got, yeah?"

Nolan glanced at the other guys on the field, most of them of average height. He'd grown accustomed to professional baseball where size often went hand in glove with talent. Six three felt average. Here, he stood a head taller than the rest.

"Let me do a few stretches, and we'll warm up."

The men darted glances between them, but no one commented. Did they not do proper stretching and warm-up routines? What kind of arm care did they have in the twenties? He couldn't remember if they had any kind of formal programs at the professional level. These guys might do anything.

"I'm Rufus." The catcher thrust his chin toward a stringy man who had to be in his thirties. "That there's Herman." Then he motioned to a boy with a mop of curly brown hair who couldn't be more than sixteen. "That's Bobby. He's Donald's nephew."

Did that mean nepotism put the boy on the team, or was he just hanging out with the men? "Nice to meet y'all. I'm Nolan Reed."

"You on the Breakers or Royal Poinciana team?" Herman, the oldest of this bunch, tugged at the laces on his glove to tighten the fingers.

Best not to mention the Brewers organization again. Nolan opened his mouth, but Pete slapped him on the back and answered for him.

"He's goin' to be one of us. Porter too."

Herman rubbed a day's growth of blond beard. Whatever he thought of that, the opinion didn't show on his face. "Glad to have you."

The men returned to their catching and throwing, though Nolan was fairly sure they kept one eye on him as he worked through his arm stretches.

When he'd limbered up, he grabbed a ball and strode to the mound. He rolled the ball around in his hand. It felt…softer than it should. Weird. The laces also felt rougher under his fingers. At what point did they change from the dead-ball era? This year or later into the twenties?

At some point, they'd outlawed spitballs and other alterations pitchers used to do to make the ball harder to hit. There'd been some kind of change with the cork center in the twenties too, but he couldn't remember what. Doubtful a hotel team had the newest balls anyway.

Rufus put on a catcher's mask and settled into position behind the plate. "Ready yet?"

Nolan aimed for the outstretched mitt and lobbed an easy throw. It hit the mitt with a solid *swack*. When Rufus tossed it back, Nolan pulled into the windup again. This time he put more heat on the ball. Three-quarter speed.

Swack.

He flexed his fingers. Still no pain. He snagged the ball from the catcher and set his feet. Probably should do more warm-up pitches to loosen his arm, but what did he have to lose in this alternate reality? His arm was fine. How that worked, he had no idea, but he might as well go with it.

Time to let 'er fly.

Fastball. Up the gut. He spun his fingers on the laces and drew his body into the windup. Weight in his rear leg.

His arm came up, and he threw all his six-three, two-hundred-thirty-pound frame through the ball. Blood rushed to his fingertips as the laces rocketed away.

Swack!

Rufus jumped to his feet and tossed the mask on the ground. "Sakes alive, fella. Can you always throw like that?"

Nolan shrugged. "Usually. The heater is usually ninety-six. Can be ninety-eight on a good day."

"What'd he say?" Pete paused at first base and cocked his head.

"Did you say ninety-eight?" Rufus spat more amber liquid. "Ninety-eight what?"

Seriously? The other men had all come closer now, watching. "Um, miles per hour."

Silence.

Then Pete threw his head back and howled. "Listen at him. Ain't no shyness in this one, eh? Where'd you come up with that, huh? Ninety miles an hour. What'd you do, get a measuring stick and a counter? I think you got your math wrong there, bucko. Ninety-eight miles an hour. What's that, like all sixty feet in less than an eye blink?"

Close enough. Nolan scratched the back of his head. Guess no radar guns these days.

Rufus removed his mitt and rubbed his palm. "You catch that ball and tell me if you don't believe it."

"Bet I can hit it outta this park." Pete called over his shoulder, already jogging toward the dugout.

"Dime says I hit it further than you!" A grin split the otherwise serious nature of Herman's face, and he broke into a jog after Pete.

The other guys followed, and soon Nolan had a line of batters ready to take a go at him. He settled into position as Pete planted his feet in the box.

Batter up. Time to work.

His heartbeat galloped into overdrive. Weird. His muscles bunched and twitched. He tried to shove the odd sensation away, but it persisted.

Find the mitt. He forced his focus away from the batter and to the padded leather target. *Breathe.*

Phantom pain scorched through his arm. The ball flew wide. Rufus dove, but the ball hit the dirt way outside. Nolan rubbed his elbow. Not real pain. He was fine. So, what *was* that?

The next pitch hit the dirt at Pete's feet. Ball three almost took off the man's knee. If he hadn't leapt backward, he'd be nursing that bruise for a while. Plenty of velocity, but no control.

Not good. What was wrong with him?

Nolan clenched his teeth as he spun the ball in his glove. He'd lost the fastball. Maybe try the sinker? Index and middle fingers gripping the laces, he settled into the windup again.

Failure punched him in the gut as soon as the ball left his hand. Too high. It sailed past Rufus's head and smacked into the stands. Nolan withheld a groan.

Pete tapped the bat on the base. "Ho, now Reed. I ain't that intimidating, am I?"

"Breeze off." Herman nudged Rufus with the end of his bat. "That's ball four. I'm up."

Pete didn't budge. "Aw, come on. Give me another go."

Herman waited, his gaze never wavering.

"Fine." Pete trudged toward the end of the line. "Maybe he'll give *you* something to hit. But that don't make our bet fair. We both gotta have a chance for it to count."

He shot Nolan a look like he'd thrown wild pitches on purpose.

Get it together. He couldn't be psyching himself out in his own dream, could he?

The next two pitches said otherwise. He had as much control as a little leaguer who couldn't hit the flat side of the concession stand.

After ball three, Rufus stood and whispered something to Herman. Herman shot Nolan a look. Then he stepped

73

out of the box. Rufus knelt into position and knuckled the mitt. Universal sign for "let it fly."

Prickles ran along Nolan's skin. *Focus on the target.*
Swack.

Rufus tossed the ball back. Next pitch. Two more. All three hit the mitt with the same satisfying sound. Without a word, Rufus nodded Herman back into the box.

Nolan hit him square in the shoulder.

Herman grunted and stepped out of the box, face reddening.

"My bad." Nolan rubbed his elbow, though it felt fine. "I don't know what the problem is today."

"Well if you ain't, I sure am." The young one, Bobby, tapped his cap on his knickers. "He's a scaredy cat. Soon as a man is in the box, he can't keep it straight."

A defense about the no-hitter he'd been chasing in his last game—the one in the future—died on his lips. The boy wasn't wrong. Soon as a man stepped into the box, he lost control. Why?

Rufus pressed his generous lips into a line. "That why you aren't playing for a real team, even with how hard you can throw?"

He did play for a real team. Not that he could tell them. He opted for a shrug.

Pete jogged to the mound and clapped his shoulder. "Aw, don't be glum. I bet we got a few tricks up our sleeves to work those jitters right out of you."

Nolan cocked an eyebrow as the other guys laughed.

"What you goin' to do?" Rufus shot Pete a wry look. "Slosh him up with hooch?"

Pete wrinkled his nose. "And make him see double so's he tries to kill both of me? I ain't no fool."

The balmy Florida heat snaked down Nolan's back in trails of sweat as the men continued to jest about all kinds of ways to loosen him up. He barely heard them. Had he lost his game? He'd seen pitchers lose their edge. There were plenty enough sob stories about pitchers who got into their heads and lost their arm in the process. But had that happened to him? All because of one insignificant injury?

Was that what this time warp was showing him?

His stomach coiled into a knot as the other men gathered around him with encouraging words and random advice that buzzed though his ears but didn't hit home.

If he didn't get his arm under control, would his career be shot?

Eight

No reason to panic. Amelia kept Tita's gaze even as her stomach clenched. It would be fine. She'd managed to keep herself under control and hadn't suffered the embarrassment of losing her lunch. Not that she'd had any. They'd spent every moment in frenzied preparation of an endless variety of breakfast treats, savory meats, fruit trays, salads, seafood towers, soups, and at this point, she couldn't even remember what else. The activity had distracted her enough to keep her mind off the frightening reality.

Until now.

"What do you mean you don't have a place to stay?" Tita tossed her apron into a basket at the rear of the kitchen, her part of the day's work finished. "Did you not set up lodging when you took the job?"

Amelia loosened her own apron and dropped it into the hamper. How did she respond to that? She'd never applied for this job, and her name wouldn't show up on any of the hotel's employment records. She'd popped right into the past without any consideration for what she'd do when she got here.

If she ever saw that creepy woman from the inn again, they were going to have a serious conversation about time-napping. She couldn't zap people through time without warning or provisions. The thought of the inn brought with it the image of Mamá's face, and tears burned behind her eyes.

How did she get out of here?

Tita's gaze roamed the spotless kitchen they'd left for the next crew. Already voices for the dinner team echoed down the hall. The morning shift handled the pastries, brunch, and luncheon, while the other crew would serve the fine dining for the fabulously wealthy.

"Yes, I suppose Rico will say that is for the best."

What? Amelia forced her attention back to the woman watching her. She'd missed whatever the woman had said. "What's for the best?"

"*Pobre chica*." Tita clucked her tongue. "You come with me. I cannot leave you on your own, I suppose."

Her tone indicated Amelia was a lost puppy who didn't have enough sense not to wander into the road. Ordinarily, she'd come up with some type of argument to prove her competence, but she couldn't seem to get enough brain cells to function.

Tita led her from the kitchen and past staff members whom she greeted. Then they exited through a side hallway and out a back door. They turned down a sidewalk lined with graceful palms and the heady scent of flowering bushes Amelia couldn't begin to name.

Wait. "What about Nolan?"

"Who?" Tita didn't pause, her steady gait pulling them farther from the hotel.

"My friend. The one who came here with me."

Tita stopped so suddenly Amelia almost ran into her. "You came here together? With a man? A man who isn't your husband?"

She blinked. "It's not like that. We've been friends my entire life. His family lived next to mine. He and my brother..." Her throat constricted. "He was my brother's best friend."

Hawklike brown eyes zoned in on Amelia as though Tita could see past Amelia's words and straight into her thoughts. "Hmm. More is there than friendship, I think."

Maybe she *could* see into her thoughts. Was that a blood thing since they were related?

Tita hurried on, leaving Amelia no choice but to follow.

"He also won't have anywhere to go." Mamá would scold her for the rudeness about to leave her lips, but it couldn't be helped. Desperate times and all that. "Were you planning on making supper...?"

"Now she invites more mouths to *cenar*." Tita wagged her head but paused at a worked-iron gate in a low wall. "Where is this boy of yours now?"

"I don't know."

Eyebrows inched toward her hairline. "Fine. You find him. Then you can both come." She adjusted the cuff on her sleeve. "We are simple people with a humble home and plain food. But you are welcome at our table to share what is ours."

Warmth seeped through Amelia's core. She grabbed Tita's hand and squeezed her fingers. "Thank you. I'm grateful for your hospitality."

Tita grunted. "Go over the bridge. Then eleven blocks east, two more south. House *número doce* on Providence

Street." She pointed a finger. "I will serve *comida* at exactly five thirty. If you are not there on time, you do not eat."

"Yes, ma'am."

Her lips twitched into what looked suspiciously close to a smile. "*Muy bien.*"

She closed the gate, and Amelia listened to the click of her heels down the sidewalk before running her hands down the pink dress hanging from her frame. Why did Mrs. Easley think she cared for pink?

Not that she'd been asked her preferences for any of this.

Squaring her shoulders, she forced herself not to think about her odd situation and set out to find Nolan. He'd said something about baseball. But that didn't make sense. Why would a hotel have a baseball team?

At the front of the sprawling structure, she found a gaggle of young men in red uniforms opening doors and ferrying luggage for couples exiting antique cars. Well, the vehicles were new during this time period. But they were those odd topless types with big fenders and a crank handle in the front. Drivers exited and opened rear doors for men in pressed suits and women in beaded dresses and funny little hats.

So weird. But kind of pretty. She frowned down at her plain frock. How come she hadn't been given one of those elegant gowns?

"Excuse me? Are you lost?"

Amelia turned toward a masculine voice belonging to a stout man in a red uniform that must be far too hot for this climate.

Lost? Ridiculously lost, if one considered both time and location. "Um, no. I don't think so. I'm looking for my friend."

The middle-aged man darted a glance at a couple swishing toward where they stood and clutched her elbow. He drew her to a far corner of the entry where the employees huddled behind what looked to be a valet station. "Who is your friend?"

"Nolan Reed. He, uh..." She notched her chin. So what if she sounded stupid? It wasn't like she'd see these people again. "He plays on the baseball team."

That last part came out a bit more like a question than she'd intended.

The man grunted. "Yes. He was late to his duties."

What did that have to do with baseball? "Do you know where I can find him?"

"Working, I should hope." He narrowed brown eyes at her. "You'll need to wait until he has completed his hours before socializing, miss."

"Oh, of course. I'm sorry."

The man's features softened. "Very good. He will be finished with his shift at five in the afternoon." He fiddled with a gold button on his jacket. "In order to attend practice, of course."

Another car puttered underneath the overhang, and a couple exited, this one with a little boy in tow. With his tailored suit and tiny hat, the kid was a miniature replica of his father. The mother, thin as a twig with golden chin-length hair, placed a gloved hand on the man's arm as they strode toward the door.

Amelia tugged her gaze away from the family and focused on the man watching her gawk. "Practice? You mean for baseball?"

No. Nolan wouldn't be staying for that, right? They had to figure out how to get home. Never mind she'd worked in a kitchen most of the day and had made supper plans. They *had* to eat. He didn't have to practice baseball.

The man's lips folded into his jowls as he pressed them into a line.

Right. She'd asked about baseball, and now she sounded like she'd lost half her brain. "Sorry. I mean, I didn't know there was a practice tonight. I was hoping he'd want to eat with me."

A twinkle entered the man's eyes. "I'm sure he would love to join you, miss. But I further imagine he'd also like to keep his employment."

Nothing she could say would make sense to this man, so she thanked him for his time and located a nearby bench to wait. She settled herself onto the slats before she noticed he'd followed her.

"We do like the main entrance to remain open for the guests."

Amelia glanced at the four other open benches. "There's plenty of room."

He shifted his weight. "Yes, miss. But the grounds are for guests only."

Oh. She rose and brushed her hands down her dress. She wasn't fancy enough to be seen hanging around. What if they were stuck here overnight? They wouldn't get to take rooms in the hotel. What was it Tita had said? Something about where the kitchen girls stayed. "Do you know anything about employee housing?"

His forehead crinkled. "Do you work here?"

"Started in the kitchen this morning." She held his long look.

What? Did he think she made it up?

"Many of the young ladies procure rooms at Mrs. Hemsley's boarding house across the bridge."

He turned as someone called out to him and scuttled away without waiting for a response.

She fiddled with her elbow-length sleeve. There had to be an employee area somewhere inside, right? With a restroom? She hadn't been all day. Maybe a break room where she could hang out without offending anyone with her presence.

What time was it, anyway? With no watch and no cell, she couldn't tell. She'd have to hope she wouldn't be stuck waiting on Nolan for too long.

The man she'd spoken to fawned over a particularly popular couple who had exited a shiny blue car with round headlights, whitewall tires, and a convertible top. The three younger bellhops edged closer, their focus darting between the tall man in a straw hat and the beauty on his arm to the rumbling horseless carriage that was probably worth a fortune in this time.

Edging her way around behind the bellhop stand, Amelia slipped to the door and let herself inside without notice.

Oh boy.

The soaring ceiling dripped with chandeliers reaching down to caress vibrant floral arrangements with their twinkling lights. Lush carpet ran the length of a hallway flanked on one side by windows she had to crane her neck to be able to see the arched tops. People gathered in clusters of three or four, all dressed in suits and gowns.

No wonder the man outside didn't want her hanging around. She was like a pizza bagel bite on a tray of French hors d'oeuvres. Better find someone in a uniform if she wanted to locate the employee area.

A form moved through the crowd, a head taller than everyone else. She'd know those wide shoulders anywhere.

Nolan.

She darted around a man with an unlit cigar hanging from his lips and hurried after him. Nolan's long stride forced her to pick up the pace as he turned a corner. She careened around the bend after him and hit something solid.

"Oh!" Amelia caught herself and grabbed the woman she'd bumped into. "So sorry."

The woman spluttered behind her, but Nolan was already disappearing down the hall, suitcase in each hand. She broke into a jog. Should she call out to him?

He turned another corner. Ugh. How big was this place? She jogged past a line of numbered doors and around the turn Nolan had taken. In time to see him push open a door with his foot and move inside.

"Wait!"

She hit the door before it could click closed and stumbled inside.

"Amelia?" Nolan dropped the two suitcases on the thick carpet. "What are you doing in here?"

"I was..." Her attention slid from him to her surroundings. "Man. What a room."

The blue-and-white theme carried from the carpet to the bedspread to the curtains fluttering in the ocean breeze. A short couch draped itself between the open curtains, the perfect place to relax and enjoy the pristine ocean view. She skirted around Nolan and plopped on the couch.

"I don't think we should be in here." He scratched the back of his head, gaze darting from the cute writing table to her and then to the door.

She pulled in a long breath of the briny breeze dancing through the window. "Who cares? If you're right, then we are time traveling to the past. So what if we sit in an empty hotel room?"

"It won't be empty long. The guests are coming." He mumbled something else she didn't catch as he opened a luggage rack and settled a leather suitcase on top of it.

Amelia swept to her feet. "What are you doing?"

"Situating the luggage. Then getting out before the people get here." He swung the other suitcase to a low bench at the foot of the plush bed. "Let's go."

He wore one of those stuffy uniforms the guys outside had worn, except his was too short in the sleeves and two inches too high over his loafers. They mustn't have many men his height working here.

"I mean what are you doing working as a bellhop?" She crossed her arms. "It doesn't make sense."

He regarded her with those dazzling eyes every girl in high school had wanted to dive into and swim around in. Then he shoved his hands in his pockets with a shrug. "It's the job they gave me."

She took another step closer. "So? That doesn't answer my question about *why* you are doing it."

His Adam's apple bobbed. "All the ballplayers work here."

"But you don't." Another step closer. Now she had to tilt her chin to study the strange way his eyes flickered. What was he hiding?

"Babe Ruth is coming." He rubbed the back of his neck, then grasped both of her shoulders. "Isn't that worth seeing?"

He smelled like fresh grass, sunshine, and childhood. Or maybe that was only the memories he stirred. Of carefree kids climbing trees, drinking from the water hose, and him and her brother chasing her with frogs.

Something in his expression changed. A subtle shift of his mouth. The slight lowering of his lids. What was he thinking about? Was he remembering those days as well? Or...what had they been talking about? Oh. Right. Baseball.

"Amelia?"

"Yes?" Why did that word come out all breathy? Like she was still a freshman with a crush. She should step away before he read every thought in her head.

Did his head lower closer to hers? She swallowed.

"Were we going on a date? Like, a real one?"

Yes. No. She'd hoped so. Maybe.

None of those words came out of her mouth. Her lips parted so at least something could seep out, but every one of them froze on her tongue. Why was he looking at her like that? Did he *want* it to be a date? Or was he once again trying to let her down easily like he'd had to do when she'd been a goofy fifteen-year-old?

His head lowered a fraction more.

Oh. Oh wow. Was he thinking of kissing her? That would change everything. Their friendship. They had history and...

All rational thought slipped away, and her chin tilted. Her eyelids drifted closed.

Then the door banged open.

Nine

Nolan maintained a gentle grip on Amelia's shoulders to keep the moment from slipping away. The guests couldn't have waited another five minutes?

"What is going on here?" A man in a white linen suit with a straw hat jammed over dark hair glared with equally dark eyes from the doorway.

Amelia tugged away from him, focus glued to the carpet.

"I've set your luggage there." Nolan nodded toward the suitcase he'd placed on the collapsible stand. "We'll be going now."

A woman in a flimsy dress covered in beadwork smirked as her blue eyes slid over him. A lioness looking for a plaything.

He took Amelia's hand and urged her toward the door, her palm hot against his.

"Don't think you'll be getting a tip after that behavior." The man turned up a thin nose as Nolan attempted to scoot past him.

"Of course, sir. Have a good day."

The man grunted as they escaped into the hallway. Just before the door shut, the woman said something about remembering what it was like to be young.

His heart pounded like this was the bottom of the ninth, two outs, and the other team was down to their last strike. Talk about terrible timing. Had he really almost kissed Amelia Cabrera?

They hurried away from the room and to the far end of the hallway, stopping at a door that must lead outside. Wainscoting lined walls topped with floral-patterned paper. Voices drifted from somewhere nearby, but for the moment, they were alone.

Amelia looked up at him, cheeks flushed. "I wanted to ask you to come to supper with me."

His scalp tingled. "Any time. Is it a date?"

She smoothed her palms down a flouncy pink dress matching the current shade of her cheeks. "It's at Tita's house." Her lashes fluttered. "Across the bridge."

"Okay." He captured her gaze. Something had almost happened back there. Something he hadn't let himself think could ever be a possibility with Derick's little sister. Were they going to talk about it? Pick up where they left off? She seemed flustered, so maybe it had been a mistake. But if that was true, then why had she just asked him out?

"Why are you looking at me like that?" Owlish eyes blinked at him.

"Like what?" He couldn't keep the smile from his voice.

She puffed out her cheeks. Did she know how cute she looked right now?

"That man said you have baseball practice." She shook her head, sending silky hair over her shoulder. She jabbed a finger at him. "Why do you have baseball practice, Nolan?"

Interesting. The unflappable Amelia Cabrera was scrambling to talk about anything other than what had almost transpired.

He fingered a lock of her hair and let it slide over his thumb. She sucked in a quick breath but didn't move away from him. "That's how it works here." He let the words glide as slowly as the strands over his fingers. "There are two hotel teams, and the rosters also work for the hotel. They put on games for the guests."

Sunlight played through the window by the door, creating caramel highlights in her hair. Would it be inappropriate if he asked if he could kiss her right here in the hallway?

"Fine. But why are *you* doing it? And wearing that uniform?" Tears glistened in her eyes, knocking away the haze that had been drifting through his brain. "Why are we *here*?"

The crack in her voice sent a punch to his gut. Here he was entertaining romantic thoughts when she hadn't been flustered by him at all. This whole situation and crazy circumstance had been too much for her. Her perfect calm had cracked around the edges, and he'd gone and heaped on more confusion.

Forcing aside all thoughts of romance, he wrapped her in a friendly hug. "I have no idea. But it's going to be okay."

After a moment, he released her and leaned against the wall, putting a safe distance between them while she gathered herself. If he could find any answer to give, he would. But no explanation made any sense. Having her look to him for comfort he couldn't provide slammed like a spear of ice through his chest.

"I want to go home."

Unable to bear even the small distance between them, he took her hand and caressed her knuckles with his thumb.

"How about we go to the front desk and see if they can help us?"

Lame. Why would the front desk be able to do anything about time travelers?

Her nose wrinkled, and she slid her hand from his. "What good will that do? What, we walk up and say, 'Excuse me, we are time travelers from the future. Do you know how to send us home?'"

A wry smile tugged his lips. "I was thinking more along the lines of asking if they had any paperwork about our employment."

"Why would they have that?"

He shrugged. Because at least it was something they could do. A tiny chance there might be a clue about why they were here. "Why did all these people expect me to be here?"

"Yeah, okay." She pulled her lower lip between her teeth. "At least it's something."

When she sucked in a breath, squared her shoulders, and strode down the hall, he pushed off the wall to follow her. At least she had some of her confidence back. They made their way through the hotel's long hallways and to the main check-in area where they located the concierge desk.

Amelia marched up to the stand and placed both hands on the polished wood. "Who do I speak to about employment records?"

The older man's gray eyebrows met the small cap perched on his head. "You wish to inquire after employment?"

She hesitated. "No, I already work here."

Oh boy.

Nolan stood beside her and offered his most charming smile. "Mr. Monroe said I had some paperwork, and I'd like to look over it. I just started this morning."

The man took in Nolan's uniform and nodded.

"And this is my friend Amelia Cabrera. She started in the kitchen today working for Mrs. Cabrera."

The lines of suspicion cleared from his cleanly-shaven face. Perhaps from the shared name. "Ah. Very good, then. One moment, and I will see if Mr. Neely has anything."

The short fellow bustled through a doorway behind the desk.

"This is crazy." Amelia crossed her arms, all evidence of the vulnerable woman from a few minutes ago gone. "You know that, right? None of this is real. Can't be."

The people buzzing around the room looked real. Cigar smoke and perfume seemed tangible. He scratched the back of his neck. Sure, it didn't make any sense, but there wasn't much point in denying they were here.

Why, well, that was another matter.

The concierge reemerged with an envelope and handed it to Nolan. "This is marked for two new employees bearing your names." He smiled. "Good day to you."

Nolan thanked the man and nodded for Amelia to follow him. Probably best if they went to that employee break room Presley had shown him. When was that? Just this morning?

They passed through the door and down the plain hallway to the small room with the big coffee jugs.

Amelia bustled to the stack of mugs and poured herself a cup. "Want one?"

"No thanks." He opened the envelope and dumped the contents onto the table. Two sheets of paper and a smaller envelope marked with their names.

Amelia peered around him as he skimmed the first page.

"Looks like this is our employment details." The page listed his name, age, and home state of Mississippi. He chuckled. "I get paid twenty cents an hour plus tips for carrying luggage and a weekly stipend of twenty-five dollars to play ball."

"I know inflation is a thing, but man." She blew on her coffee and then took a sip. "Are you sure you want to work for twenty cents an hour?"

He slid her page from under his and held it out. "You only make ten."

"What?" She snatched the page. "I make half of what you do? Unacceptable. Culinary art takes a heap more skill than hauling suitcases."

Nolan placed the two pages on the table and picked up the envelope. "I thought you said we don't work here. So what does it matter?"

She swatted him. "It's the principle."

He opened the other envelope. "Huh. It's a letter."

"Let me see." She thunked the mug onto the wooden table, sending droplets splattering. "It's from Mrs. Easley!"

He tugged his gaze away from her wide eyes and focused on the page as they read the few short lines together.

Hello, my dears!

By now, you must have realized you've been chosen for a grand adventure! That is the nature of The Depot, you see. My guests receive the unique blessing of visiting another time and place to make important discoveries. Isn't it exciting? Do make the most of the opportunity, my dears. You wouldn't want to let such an offering go to waste. It comes with many benefits, as I am sure Mr. Reed has already discovered. Have fun, learn all you can, make bold choices, and enjoy the adventure!

See you when you return.

Your friend,

Mrs. Easley

"Wow." Nolan turned the page over, but there weren't any further explanations. "That proves the time travel theory."

He'd already come to that obvious conclusion, but the letter squashed any lingering doubt. And the inn worked as some kind of time-traveling portal?

Uh-oh. What about Mrs. Cabrera? Had she traveled somewhere else? He pressed his lips together. No sense in alarming Amelia when she was already—

"This is terrible!" She flung out a hand, knocked into the barely touched mug, and sloshed coffee onto the tile floor.

Nolan grabbed a towel from the serving table to wipe up the mess. He sopped up the brown liquid and tried to keep his voice as soothing as possible. "Why? It's pretty cool. Think of it as a special vacation."

"Are you serious?" She tapped her foot right next to the last of the spill. "This isn't a vacation. It's a nightmare."

He rose and deposited the towel on the table, then wiped his hands with a napkin. "You get a chance to cook with your ancestor. What's so bad about that?"

Her forehead creased before she forced it smooth with obvious effort. "We don't belong here. That's what. What if we do something and change history? Or erase ourselves?"

"I doubt we can do that."

"It happens in the movies."

"This isn't the movies."

"Might as well be." She glowered at him. "It feels more like fiction than real life."

She had a point. But still, he couldn't muster the anxiety he should be feeling. Instead, a calming purpose blanketed his spirit. He couldn't explain it. But gut instinct shouted this could be a good thing. If they let it.

"Maybe sometimes we don't have all the answers. Maybe we have to take it with a little faith."

Something flickered through her eyes he couldn't place, but then it disappeared behind another pointed stare. She added thrusting a finger at him for good measure. "You *want* to be here."

"I'm not opposed to it."

"Why?"

Because his arm didn't hurt. Because he was going to see Babe Ruth. And because, most of all, he'd somehow managed to get what could be a romantic adventure with the one girl he'd always dreamed of but had been too chicken to pursue. Maybe here, outside of the confines of regular life, they could see what might spark between them.

None of that exited his lips. He splayed his fingers. "We're here. So why not make the most of it?"

He could practically see her brain going through the windup. Any second now, she'd let loose a curveball. "Why isn't your arm still injured? That right there is proof this isn't real, right? I mean, does time traveling heal you?"

"How should I know?" He flexed his hand. "But at least it doesn't hurt. My game is off, but my arm is fine."

"What do you mean your game is off?"

He waved the question away. They didn't need to worry about that right now. He picked up the letter. "Look, this says we went back in time for an adventure. We're supposed to make some discoveries. How about we focus on that? I bet, once we do, we'll go back home."

She notched a hand on her hip. "Since when did you become so whimsical? This is real life, Nolan."

Maybe. Maybe it was just a crazy dream. And if that was the case...

Before he could stop himself, he tossed the letter aside and swept her into his arms. His heart thudded against his chest. She'd asked him a million questions he couldn't answer. Now he'd ask one of his own.

"Were you going to go out on a real date with me?"

She blinked. Then her chin lowered in a single nod.

"And you *wanted* to go on a date with me? Knowing it would mean exploring something more than a friendship?"

She swallowed, then pulled in a long breath. Three short nods this time.

His pulse thrummed through him and made his fingers tingle. He caressed her cheek. "Is it all right if I kiss you?"

Her eyes widened and her lips parted.

Silence hung for an excruciating heartbeat. He was asking too much. Moving too fast. Too much happening right now to expect her to be able to—

She pushed up on her toes, and her lips brushed against his. Sweet. Tender. Featherlight. His arm tightened around her waist, and he snugged her closer.

Gently, slowly, he let his lips linger on hers.

And every doubt he'd ever had that Amelia couldn't be his perfect someone melted away.

Ten

Her insides bubbled like an Italian grandma's Bolognese. Despite Amelia's determined effort to shake off the effects of Nolan Reed's kiss, her senses refused to return to normal. Her face had remained heated as she'd waited for him to finish his shift. When he'd skipped practice and offered that knee-puddling smile, her mouth refused to form proper words. Her palms sweated the entire time they'd strolled down the tree-lined avenues and left the opulence of Palm Beach for the cozy homes nestled together across the bridge in West Palm Beach.

Now, as they turned on the correct street—the irony of the name hadn't been lost on her—she still couldn't get that fluttering sensation in her center to quiet.

"Providence Street, huh?" Nolan wiggled his eyebrows. "How fitting."

Did that mean because of the time travel or...no. That was silly. One kiss did not destiny make. Good gravy. She needed to get control of herself.

"We are looking for number twelve." She quickened her pace. "We better hurry. Tita said if we're late we don't eat."

Nolan easily matched her stride as they passed quaint homes, most without cars parked in the driveways. "Too bad we don't have something to bring. My mom always said you should bring a gift when invited to dinner."

Mrs. Reed did have good manners. What would she think about what had happened between her son and her son's best friend's sister? Better not linger too long on that thought. "I think Tita will understand. She's taken pity on us."

"Are you going to tell her who you are?"

Amelia stopped short in front of a low brick wall cradling an adorable bungalow with two palm trees in the yard. "Are you crazy? You think I can say, 'Hey, guess what? I'm your great-great-great-something-granddaughter?' She already thinks I'm weird."

The grin that spread across Nolan's face warned her too late he'd been messing with her. She should have caught it in his tone. But who could blame her for being too distracted by her out-of-whack thoughts to notice the obvious? She cleared her throat. "You do know this isn't a game, right?"

Broad shoulders lifted beneath the white shirt he'd worn under his red uniform jacket. "Yeah, sure. But that doesn't mean we can't enjoy what we've been given. How many people get to experience a miracle like this? It's totally cool."

Amelia brushed her hands and then straightened her spine. "Call it a miracle if you want, but I'm still calling it a nightmare."

His warm fingers slid across her palm, and her breath seized faster than a chocolate sauce over a roaring flame. "You really think that?"

With her heart beating so hard, pressure built within her like a cooker without a steam-release valve. "Well, no. But I mean. You know. It's not normal."

"So what? Normal is boring. I, for one, will take walking down a pretty street holding hands with you over sitting alone in my room nursing a wounded arm and my shredded pride any day."

What did he mean about shredded pride? Her grip on his hand tightened. "I know having your arm not hurt must be awesome."

"But...?"

"But I'm struggling with the whole concept of being…" She flapped her other hand at the cute cottage painted a charming blue as though it could encapsulate everything about 1920. "Here."

"You always do that, you know." His soft words floated through her ears and nipped at her heart.

She knew what he meant. "Do what?"

His thumb glided back and forth across her knuckles. "You're afraid of opportunities. You're scared to take risks. You'd rather hang back and stay in the familiar."

"That's hardly fair." The words shot from her lips. "I moved to Atlanta to try to get a very prestigious job. That was a risk." And a catastrophe.

She stalked down the sidewalk, but with him holding fast to her hand, she couldn't leave her mortification at being such a monumental failure behind.

"And now you're afraid to take another risk, since the last one—the only big one ever, if I'm not mistaken—didn't turn out like you'd hoped." He slowed his steps and nodded toward a house with a low stone wall and an inset iron gate. A metal 12 hung near the latch.

Cold fingers slid around her heart and squeezed. Was she that obvious? She swallowed and ended up taking in too much air. Her throat constricted and she coughed.

"Are you okay?" He patted her back, then made slow circles as she tried to catch her breath.

Sweet, but that didn't help. His touch only addled her more.

After what seemed like several minutes to her flustered brain, Amelia regained control over herself. "Swallowed down the wrong pipe, I guess. Let's go."

He didn't move. "If you don't take risks, then what happens if you miss out on something that could be amazing?"

Did he mean taking a risk with him? Risk their friendship to see if they could be something more? What if that went up in flames? She'd lose him. Could she stand them awkwardly avoiding one another for the rest of their lives? Or worse, never seeing him again? It would be terrible.

Unless...it wasn't.

Those inviting eyes called to her. They spoke of adventure and romance and...home. Like a warm blanket on a cold night. A blanket to a woman who'd been standing in an industrial freezer for hours. Or no, they invited her closer like a molten chocolate cake. Indulgent, delicious, and...

Oh dear.

That tug on one side of his lips said he could read every crazy thought zipping through her brain. She'd completely lost herself, and he knew it.

Maybe it didn't matter. Maybe the crash at the bottom would be worth the thrill of jumping off the cliff. At least she might see what it felt like to fly. This recipe—the two of them—could turn out worse than pickle and onion ice cream.

Or it might be the sweetest thing she'd ever experienced.

"You two *tortolitos* going to stand here all night and let mi amor's temper grow hot while her food grows cold?" Rico's laughing voice made Nolan startle.

Red crawled up Nolan's neck as he scratched the back of his head, his eyes apologetic even though he didn't release her hand. Or stop staring at her like that. Even with his limited Spanish, he must know what tortolitos meant.

Lovebirds.

She opened her mouth to refute the claim, to say they were friends and nothing more, but she snapped her teeth together before the words could pop free.

Hurting Nolan with such a careless dismissal?

That wasn't a risk she was willing to take.

The Cabrera house smelled like home. Not *his* home, but since Nolan had been best friends with Derick since he was four, he'd spent enough time in the Cabrera household for it to count as a close second. This reminded him of long summer nights with churros, empanadas, and contagious laughter.

He followed Amelia through the door to a vibrant blue room that suited the home's occupants. Gone was the drab dress and apron he'd seen Amelia's ancestor in earlier. Tita's multicolored skirt brushed the tops of heeled shoes, and the yellow blouse washed the room in sunshine. The man on her arm had a smile bright enough to light a stadium. His simple brown trousers and white shirt might have seemed subdued on a less animated man.

"Come in, come in!" Mr. Cabrera extended his hand and introduced himself to Nolan, then slapped his palm to his heart. "Ah, and here is the señorita who did not bring me my treat this morning."

Tita rolled her eyes.

A teasing smile tilted Amelia's lips. "Then I will have to bring you double tomorrow."

"Ah! I knew I would like this one." Mr. Cabrera—Rico—tapped the tip of his nose. "It must be in the name, sì? We are a people of wit and good humor."

What would he think if he knew the truth about Amelia? Nolan slid a glance her way. Her eyes laughed, but sadness lowered her smile.

Rico laughed, deep and rich, at something his wife said about him poorly representing said name. He laughed like Manuel. Amelia's father. In fact, add a few years and gray hairs and the resemblance was uncanny.

"Come!" Tita smacked her hands together. "We don't want it to get cold."

Too bad Nolan didn't have some flowers or something to give her. Good manners were the best he could do. "*Gracias por tu hospitalidad.* I don't know where I would have gotten supper tonight."

Her eyes widened for only a second before her cheeks lifted. "Ah, a good boy. Your Mamá must have taught you well."

They followed the couple past a cozy sitting area with worn but colorful furniture and into a warm kitchen brimming with delights that made his stomach grumble. How had Tita produced the amount of food crammed onto the center of the circular table in such a small space?

Six chairs huddled around a wooden table that hefted four table settings on yellow place mats and no less than seven platters of food.

"Empanadas?" His mouth watered. "Oh, and is that ropa vieja?"

Rico poured ice water into the glasses on the table. "The boy knows his Latin food." He winked at Amelia. "It's no wonder you have chosen him. You will get to make plenty of big meals for him, yes?"

Amelia chuckled. "Sì, he has always loved my family's cooking." She swallowed. "My father used to cook for us all of the time."

Nolan pulled a chair out for Amelia, which earned an approving look from her great-grandmother. Okay, well, it was her like four or five greats or something, but who could keep up with that? One great was enough. For whatever reason, the woman's approval mattered. At least, it sent a satisfied tingle through him.

Rico did the same for Tita and then leveled them both with a look. "At my house, we give thanks to God for our meals. If you have issue with this, you do not need to stay."

Nolan had yet to hear the man sound so serious. Rico's gaze remained pinned to Nolan even as Nolan shot a questioning look to Amelia.

"Yes, sir." He held the man's solemn gaze. "We do the same in my family as well. I am also a man of God."

This earned another wink toward Amelia. "Excellent. You have indeed chosen well."

"Enough." Tita waved a hand at him. "You are embarrassing the *jovenes*. Let's pray."

They bowed their heads while Rico asked a simple prayer for their food and thanked God for a good day, and for a healthy family and new friends. In that, too, he reminded Nolan of Amelia's dad.

As soon as the prayer finished, Rico passed the first course. Nolan spooned marinated tomatoes and olives with herbs onto his plate and then handed Amelia the platter. Next came the rice and sautéed peppers, then the fried pies.

He bit into the flaky crust and savored the ground beef seasoned with cilantro and spices he couldn't name.

Delicious.

"See? He is too interested in eating to listen." Rico's amused words tugged Nolan from his food-induced deafness.

"Sorry. What?" He flashed a sheepish grin. "These are amazing."

"Eat." Tita's pleased expression spread to her husband, and they both reached for the plate to pass him more empanadas.

"These are very good, Tita. There's something a bit extra to them." Amelia rolled her tongue around in her mouth. "Did you use orange?"

Rico nudged his wife's shoulder. "Ah! Another with the gift. She might make as good a cook as you, mi amor, as soon as we can put a little meat on her."

"Hush, you. It's impolite to talk about a young woman's figure. She's perfectly lovely."

Rico lifted his eyebrows and passed Amelia a plate of rice. Which earned a stifled giggle from her and a glare from Tita.

The conversation turned to questions about the hotel and Amelia's experience in the kitchen, but soon the words faded into a soothing murmur.

He missed this. Family gatherings around the table. A cozy home rather than a lonely apartment. He'd thrown his entire being into pursuing his career. He believed God had called him to that profession and blessed him with the talents to accomplish it. But had he neglected everything else in his pursuit? He'd put off time with his parents because he feared spending too much time with Dad would reveal where he didn't measure up.

That was stupid. His parents had always been proud of him. Major-league career or not.

Even if he never got called up, would it be enough? Could he enjoy his time in the minor leagues and then spend his days coaching kids who loved the game like he did?

Would Amelia fit into that future?

Could they have a home like this someday? Simple and cozy, with love in abundance?

She caressed him with a lingering glance, and his insides turned.

Making it to the majors had always been his priority.

But maybe it was time to make a few adjustments.

Eleven

Make bold choices. The words from Mrs. Easley's letter pinged around in Amelia's head as she fumbled in the dark. Turned out Nolan had accommodations afforded to him for being a baseball player, but kitchen staff didn't receive such luxuries. What would she have done if not for the kindness of her ancestors who'd offered their spare room?

She'd spent the night in a cozy space her great-great-uncles used on occasion when they visited. Green walls, hardwood floors, and masculine furniture completed the no-nonsense design. The mattress had been soft, and Tita might have made that quilt herself. Not that Amelia had used it. A ninety-degree night with no air-conditioning meant she'd spent hours marinating in her own sweat.

How come Nolan had received physical healing and the chance to see one of his baseball heroes in real life while all she'd been given was a bare-bones trip to the past instead of the nice weekend she was supposed to spend with her mother? Well, maybe that wasn't fair. She had gotten to meet her great-great-great-grandparents. Not many people could say the same.

She leaned toward a silver-back mirror and tried to see herself in the flickering lamplight. Lighting it had been a feat that had taken three tries and cost a burned finger. She frowned at the dim reflection. Awful. No change of clothes, no hairbrush, no makeup.

Bold choices? The only choice she *had* was to wear rumpled clothes she'd slept in and face the day without a toothbrush or deodorant. And Nolan wondered why she wasn't psyched about this place. Still, if bold choices would get her home, then that's what she'd do.

As soon as one presented itself.

It looked like Mrs. Easley would make them stay in the past until they learned...something. Like she had a clue what it could be. Maybe her lesson had to do with Tita and her recipes. But how would she get the woman to give up family secrets without revealing their connection?

A light knock tapped at the door.

"¿Pequeña? Are you ready?" Tita's voice tugged Amelia away from the mirror and her rambling thoughts.

She opened the door and gestured to the lamp. "How do I turn it off?"

Turning the knob on the handheld lantern only increased and decreased the flame, and since a glass-bottle surrounded the wick, she couldn't blow it out like a candle. She'd had to stick the oversized match through the top—hence the scorched finger—to light it. Not that she'd needed the thing. How much light did a person require to get ready for the day when she had to keep the same clothes she'd slept in?

Tita's eyebrows inched toward her hairline. "You don't know how to blow out a lamp?"

"I'm used to electric lights." That sounded more defensive than it should have.

Tita studied her. Probably wondering why a girl accustomed to expensive electric lights couldn't afford different clothes, food, or a place to stay.

Thanks again, time warp.

Awkward silence simmered before Tita edged around her, lifted the globe off the lamp, and blew out the flame. She slid the glass back into place without a word.

Heat crept up Amelia's neck. Why hadn't she thought of that?

"Come along. We need to hurry, or we're going to be late." Tita wiggled her fingers for Amelia to follow her through the dark house.

They stepped into a morning too early for even the first rays of sunlight. "What about Rico? He's not coming with us?"

Tita inserted a lock into the front door and secured the metal latch. "He's been gone for over an hour. He likes to get an early start in the front gardens before the guests rise."

He did gardening in the dark? How did that work?

After looking stupid with the lamp, Amelia wouldn't ask. They started down the sidewalk at a brisk pace. Warm summer air glided over her face with a salty touch. The breeze smelled of ocean, flowers, and freshness. They passed several slumbering bungalows and turned off Providence Street.

"Tita, can I ask you something?" Amelia fiddled with a wrinkle on her skirt.

Overhead, untainted starlight twinkled like a million sparkles on a satin gown.

"*Por supuesto*." Tita strode through the dimly lit neighborhood, unencumbered by the lack of a flashlight. "What troubles you?"

"Do you believe in miracles?"

"Absolutely. Don't you?"

Amelia matched her stride. "I'm not talking about the kind you see in the Bible where Jesus heals blind people or the regular-life stuff people call miracles like babies being born. I mean things that are...a bit locas, I guess."

"Like what?" Equal measures of curiosity and skepticism leveled Tita's tone.

Right. Amelia walked herself into this one. "I just mean, do you think God ever does super-crazy things?"

"Like what?" This time the words held laughter.

"Oh, I don't know. Just wild, out-there things. Big things. Like sending people to see the future or something."

Tita sent her a thoughtful glance. "How should I know? Just because something like that has never happened to me doesn't mean it can't. All things are possible with God." They turned the corner. "Why? Are you praying to skip forward and see how your life turns out?"

"No." Amelia pushed a laugh from her chest, but even she could tell how forced it sounded. "Just wondering."

But that would be helpful. Too bad God didn't mail you a letter and show you all the steps you should take and save you the trouble of failing. She'd cook up whatever he wanted her to if he'd hand her a recipe.

But instead of a helpful glimpse of the future, she'd been dumped in the past.

"Life is full of unexpected things, pequeña." Tita mounted the long bridge toward the strip of beach where opulence reigned. "Do these questions have something to do with your chico?"

Her young man. He wasn't hers. Though perhaps he could be. Precarious topic, but still safer than time travel. "We've been friends since we were small. Well, he was friends with my big brother. I've known him all my life. I guess I'm worried that, if we start a romantic relationship and it doesn't work out, I'll lose him."

"A reasonable consideration." Tita patted her dark hair, though not a strand dared to fall out of place. "But let me ask you something else. What do you think makes the best foundation for love?"

The answer seemed obvious. "Friendship?"

Tita winked at her. Rico's teasing must've rubbed off. "*Exactamente.* I am not well acquainted with either of you, but it seems like you enjoy one another's company. Does your mother approve of him?"

"She loves Nolan."

"And do his parents like you?"

"I think so." She didn't know how else to answer that. She had no idea what they might think of her and Nolan dating, but Mr. and Mrs. Reed had always gotten along well with her family.

At the peak of the bridge, the natural splendor caught her. The water glistened in the moonlight, threads of silver sparkling across an indigo expanse. Her steps slowed. Yachts bobbed by their docks, the world silent and waiting for even the birds to rise.

Such beauty in creation. Why had she hardly stopped to notice it? She was always so busy, going from one place to another and—oh no.

Tita was already twenty feet away. How did that woman move so fast? Amelia scurried to Tita's side. Her ancestor resumed the conversation as though Amelia hadn't dawdled.

"Life is full of risks. You care for him, and he cares for you. Your families approve of one another. He is a man of God. Why not take a chance on him?"

Why not indeed?

Tita allowed her to mull over those implications in silence until they entered the hotel's rear gate and passed into Rico's domain.

The older man stooped in front of a rosebush, snipping dead blooms. He straightened and rubbed his back as they approached.

"I thought you took care of the front gardens in the dark." Why were those the first words to pop out of her mouth? Why not something reasonable, like good morning?

He tipped a straw hat back on his head. "I get the *chicos* started. I'll check on them again at first light. I cannot miss the arrival of mi amor and my morning *beso*."

She couldn't help but chuckle as Rico swept Tita into an embrace and placed a lingering kiss on her lips. Tita's grin could have replaced the sunrise.

Something warm settled in Amelia's stomach. Could *this* be her glimpse into her future? Could she and Nolan build an epic love like her ancestors shared? Her fingertips tingled.

Maybe this trip to the past was about her future after all.

Twelve

This was awesome. Nolan sent up a little prayer of thanks as he shucked his porter's jacket for his ball uniform. Sure, he had to lug around suitcases for part of the day. But soon enough, he'd have a ball in his hand, and—not that he wanted to jinx anything—he felt close to having the girl on his arm.

A sultry breeze blasted his face and wiggled down his jersey, cooling the sweat on his neck as he trotted from the humble locker room to the field. Grass, dirt, and sunshine. Such simple pleasures in life made a man feel alive. Well, those and the sparkle in a certain set of velvet eyes and the honey-sweet feel of silky lips.

He slid through the low gate and jogged onto the field. The full roster of men spread out into their positions, throwing warm-ups or working through drills. Each one wore the white uniform with red pinstripe he did.

Without a regular bullpen, he opted for a place by the fence to start his stretches. The balmy air smelled of freedom and opportunity. This trip was by far the best vacation. Way better recovery time than he could have dreamed. Playing ball without any pressure. Winning the girl. Seeing a legend. What more could a guy ask for?

"Hey!" The gruff shout snagged his momentum. "You got cotton in your ears or what?"

The gaze of a dozen other men drifted his way. Rufus eyed him with his catcher's mask shoved underneath one wiry arm. His pinched lips could be from annoyance or tobacco, but either way, he looked like someone sucking on a straw clogged by a lemon seed.

"Sorry." Nolan tugged the laces on his glove to check the ties. "What did you say?"

The stream of tobacco juice Rufus spat congealed in the red dirt under his feet. "I asked if you were ready."

"Need to do my stretches first."

Rufus scratched the back of his head. His mouth puckered like he meant to say something, but then thought better of it. He shrugged. "Suit yourself. Any fella who can blast it like you can has the right to his routines."

Those routines had been analyzed by professionals to help top-notch athletes perform at their peak, so yeah, he'd stick with them.

The catcher sauntered closer and lowered his voice. "Try to get some control though, eh? Don't want Adams seeing you do what you did yesterday if you have any hope of staying on this team."

Nolan followed the man's less-than-covert gaze to the dugout and had to stifle a grin. Irony always did get him. Here he was in 1920, and his ball club's manager looked like he stepped off some kind of gangster film. No zoot suit and fedora, but with his square face, shaved head, and a scowl weighing down a generous mouth, he gave off an Al Capone vibe. Not that Nolan knew much about that guy or those kinds of movies. He'd always been too busy playing ball, practicing ball, or watching ball games to be into old movies. But if he'd had to peg a man to play a guy in a black-and-white prohibition flick, this man fit.

Or maybe his imagination had gone into overdrive, given the circumstances. He flattened his mouth before anyone noticed him grinning like an idiot.

The manager caught his eye and dipped his chin, then gestured toward the mound. So much for arm care. He should have a talk with these guys about fostering longevity in players.

Still, he wouldn't sabotage his place here. Not before he got the chance to see Babe Ruth. He took the mound and set his feet.

Caution nagged him. For all his talk to Amelia about taking chances, he'd been drilled since T-ball not to be stupid with his arm. He could start with an easy long toss. He lobbed the ball to Rufus. It arched high, and the man stood to catch it.

The catcher held the ball as he jerked his eyebrows toward the dugout, his wide eyes clear as any words.

"Just warming up. You can stand until I get my arm loose." Without waiting for a response, Nolan tossed another.

They threw the ball, with Rufus growing antsier by the second, until Nolan's muscles loosed enough he shouldn't cause an injury. He wouldn't be trying for velocity today. Not until he got his mechanics back under control and could nail down his accuracy.

Didn't Mrs. Easley say they had to learn a few things here? What would be the purpose of having him on a team if it wasn't for additional field time?

With a nod to the catcher, he planted his feet on the rubber and shifted his weight into the windup.

Two-seamer up the gut.

Swack.

Four-seamer running in.

Swack.

Tension melted from his shoulders. Maybe he'd just had an off day yesterday. The stress of the unusual circumstances could do that. He'd been sucked through a time warp, after all. There wasn't anything wrong with him. He hadn't lost his edge.

He shook out his body and bounced on his toes. Yeah. That had to be it. A little extra time on the field to hone his game without losing time to an injury and extra evenings to get to know Amelia as more than friends.

"That all you got?"

The bellowed words punched through his swelling ego like a bullet through a balloon. He withheld a cringe, though only barely. He set his teeth and twisted toward the dugout.

Adams crossed his arms over a barrel chest. "These boys made it sound like you had an arm. Though with that wacky way you're throwing, it's hard to see how you're even doing as good as ya are."

Wacky? He had great mechanics. Sweat slid down his hairline. Accuracy mattered more than velocity. Plus, he didn't need to cause any injuries. But then again, how bad could it be for a miracle arm? If he didn't bring an arm injury with him, maybe he couldn't cause one either.

He nodded to Rufus. If Adams wanted to see what he could do, he'd give him a show. With a whip-crack grin, the catcher dropped into position.

Deep breath. Here came the heater.

Swack.

He resisted the urge to look at Adams as Rufus flung off the glove and rubbed his palm. After three heartbeats, a long whistle broke the silence. "Can you do that more than once?"

Rufus repositioned his glove. His Adam's apple bobbed when he gave the nod.

Nolan let it rip and hit the glove with a satisfactory *thwap*. Rufus glanced at Adams before tossing the ball back. Nolan stared at the ball in his palm. Was he throwing harder than before?

Lightning skittered through his arms. No way. What if this time-warp thing was like that movie where the kid had arm surgery and ended up playing in the big leagues because he could throw harder than Nolan Ryan?

What was he throwing now? Had he come close to his namesake's famous 108? What he wouldn't do for a radar gun.

Rufus shook his arm, the glove on the end flopping. The muscle in his jaw twitched as he lowered into the crouch.

Nolan threw everything he had into the pitch. Blood rushed through his fingertips and pulsed against the stitching leaving his hand.

Swack.

"Sakes!" Rufus popped to his feet and threw the glove in the dirt. "You're going to have to get me a thicker glove if you expect me to catch for this guy."

Nolan swiped his cap to mop the sweat from his brow.

The manager approached the mound and swept an assessing gaze down Nolan. "Where'd you come from, boy?"

The way he asked made it seem like he thought Nolan had landed here from another planet.

"Mississippi." Truthful answer, if not the whole of it.

"And what brings you here?"

How did he answer that? He shifted his feet. "I heard Babe Ruth and the Yankees are going to play here on Saturday."

Adams sucked his teeth. "Yankees fan?"

Not in the strictest sense of undying loyalty. He wouldn't be wearing their cap anytime soon, but they did have the greats. Ruth, Mantle, Berra, Jeter, and a ton of others. "Yes, sir."

Adams grunted and rubbed his hairless chin that could have been mined from a quarry. "Keep throwing like that and maybe you'll catch their eye."

His stomach clenched. Wait. Did that mean *he* could be pitching to *the* Babe Ruth?

"Managers will be poking around. They're looking into making Palm Beach a spring training location like what they do down in Miami. Maybe one of them will get a glimpse of you if you make yourself available."

Oh. Right. Of course, the big-league guys wouldn't be playing the hotel staff. But that didn't mean he couldn't catch a scout's attention. Not that he'd be signing with anyone. It would just be cool. Knowing he could have made a team with Ruth.

Nolan nodded. "Thank you, sir."

They worked through drills, did some infield work, and settled into the rhythm that had been normal since childhood.

"Line up!" Adams shouted, bringing a halt to the first base drills. "You lot are going to see if you can hit anything this farm boy can throw at you."

Farm boy? Because he was from Mississippi?

The men scrambled to the dugout and tossed down gloves. The first one crowded the batter's box a heartbeat later.

"Think you can throw me something to hit this time?" Pete waggled the bat, his good-natured teasing drawing a laugh from the others. "You ain't the only fellow wanting to impress a few Yankees you know."

Nolan's fingers tingled, and something crept up his throat. Not again. He willed his body to settle.

Just a batter up to the plate. Nothing he hadn't faced a thousand times before.

Heel against the rubber. Feel the stretch. The windup.

Breathe in.

His body mechanics took over. Coil. Rocket forward down the mound. Release.

A bullet screamed from his fingertips and over a sea of red dirt.

Oh no.

With a sickening thud, it hit Pete right in the ribs.

Thirteen

Oh no, not—again. Amelia glared at the offending contraption. "Fish sticks and feathers!"

A giggle erupted behind her, and a second later, Edna flounced to Amelia's side. The young blond wrinkled her nose. "What did you say?"

Stupid, old-fashioned, worthless, junk. She shook the mixer, sending globs of fresh cream all over the counter.

"What?" Great. Now she'd made a mess. Amelia blinked at the teen. "Oh. It's just a silly saying my dad had. I think it means something like 'this is stupidly ridiculous.'"

Edna pried the handheld mixer from her grasp. "You must be gentle. Try to go too fast, and it'll snag." She cranked the handle, and the gears rotated the whisks smoothly. But the cream didn't froth.

Amelia snatched a towel and swiped up the splatter. "This is never going to work. How am I supposed to make whipped cream without a real mixer?"

"This *is* a mixer." Edna tilted the tool to the edge of the bowl and, grasping the top handle firmly, cranked faster. The liquid began to thicken. "See? Just takes practice."

"Thanks." Amelia watched Edna work without the mechanism catching and binding. "You're good at that."

The cream frothed around the edges, and soon Edna had a smooth batch of whipped cream. "Not so hard once you get the feel for it. You spend as many days in the kitchen as I have, and you'll be able to make this in your sleep."

Amelia pressed her lips together to keep from spouting that she *had* spent countless hours in the kitchen and could present a five-star menu to the president himself. The pride drained out of her inflated ego with a simple prick of conscience. She could do that only if she had modern equipment. Did she even remember what it had been like to cook with her dad? Simple ingredients, traditional methods, and rustic food that fed the heart as well as the stomach?

She accepted the topping from the younger woman and placed it inside the icebox to keep cool. Now, where had she put those strawberries for the fruit trays?

"Oh my!" Edna gasped and skirted around where Amelia searched the countertops for something that should not be this difficult to locate.

The words registered, and Amelia's gaze followed the girl's path through the bustling kitchen. Nolan stood in the doorway with his arm supporting another man whose tight lips and pale features indicated injury.

Nolan's gaze found hers, and he mouthed, "Got any ice?"

Not in the way he would be used to. She'd discovered that inconvenience this morning. Grabbing a screwdriver thing and a dainty hammer from the drawer, she lifted the lid on a wooden box lined with metal to reveal a single hay-bale-sized block of ice. She smacked the ice pick into the glassy surface and tapped the wooden handle with the mallet. A crack formed. She tapped harder, and the pick slid to the side, skittering over the slick surface to gouge into the icebox.

Uh-oh. That pinprick hole better not be a problem. Behind her, voices tittered. Whatever had happened to Nolan's friend, it caused a stir. After several more attempts, she separated three hand-sized chunks from the block. She wrapped them in a kitchen towel to take to Nolan.

Edna had a hand on Nolan's arm, big blue eyes locked on his face. "...and a baseball can do that?"

Nolan wore guilt like a chocolate coating. It obscured almost everything about his face. He scrubbed a hand down the back of his neck. "I shouldn't have lost control. I think it's the laces."

"I brought the ice." Amelia lifted the lopsided bundle toward him, and he nodded to the skinny man slumped on the short bench by the door.

"Think that will help?" The guy's hair flopped as he shook his head at Amelia's offering. "Nolan insisted we come to the kitchen straightaway. I went along, mind, because it beats standing out in the heat with my side on fire. But I don't see how putting that chunk of ice is going to do much more than keep me from sweating."

He hadn't heard of icing an injury? That seemed unlikely. This wasn't the 1700s. Surely, they had normal first aid a hundred years ago. Rather than respond, she held the towel out to him.

Pete—she'd met him yesterday when he'd come to the kitchen to flirt with Edna and managed to charm Tita—lifted a striped uniform shirt to reveal a nasty bruise on his lower ribs. Nolan must have hit him square with one of his fastballs. Strange. He had impeccable control.

Because of that and his speed, everyone wondered why he'd been in AA for three years.

"Keep it wrapped in the towel and press it to the bruise." She wasn't a doctor or anything, but she'd seen enough of these injuries with her brother and his friends growing up. "It'll make it feel better and help with the swelling."

The other women who had craned their necks to the commotion became supremely interested in their tasks. Tita's voice came a second later. They must have heard her come through the garden door.

"What's this? What's happening?" Tita shooed girls out of her way.

Nolan ducked his head like a scolded puppy. Edna—who still hadn't removed her hand from his sleeve—stared up at him with bright eyes, while Pete stared at Edna with downturned lips. Only Amelia kept herself in check. Never mind the way her fingers twitched to swat Edna away from Nolan.

"This lout hit me instead of the catcher." Despite the words, Pete's features held only repressed pain, not animosity. "Who would have figured his crazy way of throwing would hurt so much."

"Sorry." Nolan moved to shove his hands in his pockets, but since he didn't have any, his palms slid down his pants.

At least the movement made Edna release her hold. That, and Tita's raised eyebrows.

"I am sorry for your pain, young man." Tita gestured to Edna to get back to work. "But I do not understand why it brings you to my kitchen in the middle of our busiest hour."

"That's my fault, señora." Nolan shifted his feet and didn't notice the flirty glance Edna threw over her shoulder as she took her time returning to the prep counter. "I told him the ice would help the swelling, and since there isn't any in our locker room, I came here."

Tita tilted her head. "Why would there be ice at a baseball field?" She shook away her question before they could answer. "If you have what you need, then off you go. I don't need you *desmayando chicas.*"

He was hardly making anyone swoon. Well, except Edna. What was *that* about? Sure, Nolan cut a handsome picture, but still. She'd thought Pete and Edna were a thing. At least based on how they'd acted before. Pete thought so too, given the way his longing gaze trailed her every move.

"Thanks for the ice." Nolan cupped Amelia into an awkward side hug, then released. "I better go. See you after?"

"Yeah. Tita invited me to make torticas de Morón this afternoon. Well, Rico invited me, and she didn't refuse."

Nolan chuckled. "Good. You should do stuff like that while you have the chance."

The unspoken part lingered between them. Who knew how long they'd be here. Using Mrs. Easley's antique mixer got her sent to the past but wouldn't offer round-trip fare. And who knew where Nolan would find another Babe Ruth baseball card. Maybe the man himself would send Nolan back when he came.

Oh no. What if that meant he went home, and she didn't?

Nolan trailed Pete out the door. Funny how that crooked grin had never made her stomach twist in knots before. She pushed the sensation aside and got back to work.

Several hours and an endless supply of food later, the morning shift gave way to the afternoon. After wiping down the counters and dropping their aprons in the hamper, Amelia and Tita exited the gate at the rear of the property.

Hotter today than yesterday. Sweat dampened her dress. Thankfully she couldn't smell herself, but spending all morning working in a stuffy kitchen without air-conditioning while lacking deodorant surely made for an odiferous affair.

"Are you going to tell me what's going on?"

Amelia stumbled at Tita's sudden words. Huh? Did she mean with Nolan or...? "What are you talking about?"

"There is something *raro en ti*. I would like you to tell me what it is."

Her stomach clenched. There most definitely *was* something odd about her. But who would ever believe it stemmed from being a woman out of time? She choked out a nervous laugh that did nothing to convince Tita of her ignorance of the subject. "Like what?"

Tita's eyebrows arched toward her still-perfect hair. Did the woman not sweat? "You can make the most delicious soufflé but can't turn a mixer. You are confused by an icebox and how to work a stove, yet you know how to cook. Why is this?"

How could she answer that? She quickened her pace toward the bridge.

Tita had no trouble keeping stride. "The truth, please, pequeña."

A line from that military movie—"You can't handle the truth!"—shot through her brain. She opted for a different quote instead. "Sometimes the truth is stranger than fiction."

"Ha!" Tita waggled a finger. "That may be. But truth is still better than fiction, so I'll have it now."

Fish sticks and feathers. Amelia pressed her lips together. Anything she could come up with would be an outright lie. Even if she was willing to lie to her ancestor—who had been nothing but kind and generous to her—she wouldn't be able to come up with anything plausible. Or remember it to keep up the ruse if she did. She had the imagination of a chef, not a novelist.

Tita stopped in the middle of the sidewalk and crossed her arms. "There will be no going farther until you are honest with me, young lady. Now speak."

"I'm from the future." The words popped free like warm biscuit dough out of a store-bought tube. Sticky, messy, and all out of shape.

Tita kept a level gaze on her. No reaction. Simply waiting for more.

"I'm your great-great-great-granddaughter." No response. Amelia twisted her fingers, jumbled words finding their way out of her mouth despite her brain's warning that she sounded like a madwoman. "My father was named for his grandfather, your youngest son. I came here from a time-traveling inn. I don't know why or how to go home. But I think maybe...maybe I'm here in part so that I could meet you and learn some of our family recipes. I have your book. The one with the blue flower on the front. I know the ingredients, but I can't ever get the method right."

She'd done it now. They'd kick her out. Where would she go?

Tita whirled on her heel and stalked down the sidewalk, leaving Amelia with the unfortunate dilemma of whether to follow.

Fourteen

Nolan knuckled the small of his back as Pete shot him a sour glance. "I'm telling you, it's true. Saw it with my own eyes."

In the hotel hallway, they passed a pair of female guests dressed in flowy dresses, gloves, and pearls. One of them turned up bright red lips at him.

They'd not made it four steps before Pete groused again. "See? Even the rich women look your way. What hope do I have now that you're here? She'll never notice me again."

"You're overreacting. Nothing happened."

Pete snorted. "You must be blind not to have noticed how she was moonin' over you."

The blond woman in the kitchen, the one barely out of high school at best, had been intent on asking questions, but nothing else. "She wanted to know what happened to you."

"So instead of asking me, she stood there with her hand on you and those big eyes drinking in your every word?"

Nolan kneaded a muscle tightening in his neck. "I'm not trying to get in your way, Pete. I'm not interested in Edna."

They took a turn at the next hallway. Pete gestured with the rag holding his ice, which he still carried but didn't apply to his ribs. "That makes it worse."

"Why?"

"Because you are interested in a girl who ain't interested in you, and the one who ain't interested in me is interested in you."

Good grief. "Amelia is interested in me."

Did that sound too arrogant?

"Ha! See. They all have eyes for you, and you know it."

He'd walked himself right into that one. He opened the door to the hotel break room and stepped inside. "I don't know what else to say. I'm not trying to date Edna. If you have feelings for her, then you should tell her."

"You tell your girl?"

A bubble of pride surfaced. "Kissed her yesterday."

Pete let out a low whistle and heat crept up Nolan's neck. He shouldn't have said that. Amelia wouldn't appreciate him sharing details in what equated to lock-er-room talk.

"I think she could be the one." Maybe that helped.

"Thought you said you ain't officially started seeing her like that yet." Pete sidled to the coffeepot, movements still ginger.

How did he find hot coffee appealing in this heat? "We've been friends most of our lives. I know everything I need to know about her."

"My pa said no man knows anything about a woman. And he finds out he knew even less than he thought once he marries her." Pete took a sip and eased into a chair. "But we all know one thing. They like you tall, broad types the best. Ain't no denying that one."

This conversation was running the bases in repeat. "We should get back to the team."

"I got a few more minutes." Pete stretched his arms over his head and winced.

The door behind Nolan banged open. He should have known Presley Monroe would find them in the break room and assume they shirked their work. The least he could do was take one for the team. He opened his mouth to defend their presence, but Pete dashed his chances.

"These ain't our hours, sir. The team is having practice."

"Then why are you here?" Presley punctuated each word with a jab of his finger. "Shouldn't you be on the field?"

"That's my fault, sir." Nolan stepped to where Pete nursed his mug of coffee. "I took him to get some ice after I drilled him, and we were giving it a few minutes."

The older man puffed out his jowls. "What's this now? You what? Drilled him?"

Right. Modern slang would fly right over his head. "I mean I hit him with the ball."

Monroe snorted. "That's no call for lounging. You are paid to work, not wallow like a boy with a stubbed toe. Out with you."

Getting hit with a ninety-eight-mile-an-hour fastball differed from a bumped toe. But Pete could nurse his sore ribs in the dugout. Which is where they should have returned if Nolan had been thinking properly. But Pete had been too busy complaining about being too short and skinny for the pretty girls, and Nolan had followed him here. Didn't seem right to leave him and go back to the team on his own, seeing as how he'd caused Pete's problem.

The sore ribs, at least.

Pete left the wet rag on the table and strode to the door. Looked like they'd be getting back to the team after all.

The head porter's words caught Nolan as he crossed to the door. "Don't let them who lack your ambition cost you your goals."

"Yes, sir." For some reason, the words struck deeper than they should. But he'd have to examine that later. He closed the door behind him.

Pete cut his gaze at Nolan as they ambled down the hallway. "If I'd have known the man making the throw would get the sympathy and not the fellow who'd been hit, I'd have walloped you. You need to stop that goofy way of throwing and pitch like a real ballplayer."

Would the guy never let that go? Only one woman in that kitchen held Nolan's eye, but saying so again wouldn't make a dent in Pete's determined self-degradation. Nolan focused on the other part of the complaint. "I'm not changing my mechanics. Consistent mechanics is why I can throw that hard."

They exited the hotel into the bright sunshine, and Pete tugged his cap low. "What good is throwing hard if you can't throw it right?"

He had a point. "I'm usually more accurate."

As they neared the field, excited chatter mingled with the salty air. Nolan quickened his pace. "I wonder what's going on."

Past the fence, the team gathered around the dugout, blocking Nolan's view of whatever had captured their attention within. He jerked his chin at Pete. "We better hurry. He's probably giving out the lineup or going over something important."

As they neared, parts of conversation separated from the general hum.

"I saw you pitch last season." Rufus leaned over the rail. "Really thought the Sox would get another pennant."

What was he talking about?

Pete pressed his way in between Bobby and another team member Nolan hadn't officially met.

"Is it true you hit twenty-nine home runs?" This from Bobby.

A sensation tingled along Nolan's arms. Wait. Who did they have in there? Nolan stepped closer to look down into the dugout, and his pulse skittered.

The Sultan of Swat. The Great Bambino. Here in the flesh.

Oh man.

Babe Ruth. Arguably the greatest player in baseball history. He looked exactly like Nolan expected from the old black-and-white cards. Rounded cheeks, bright eyes, and already plenty of swagger. And he hadn't even hit his prime yet. He'd racked up twenty-nine homers last season, but his first year with the Yankees would be fifty-four.

Of course, ushering in the live-ball era would help with that a lot. Cork centers in the ball and new rules that would come around this year against pitchers using the good old "spitball" or doing anything else to alter the spin would favor the hitters.

And Nolan stood right on the threshold of it all.

Wow. Thanks, God. I don't know why you decided to send me here or give me this dream or whatever it is, but thank you. This is totally cool.

"He thinks he can get one by me, you say?"

The laughed words, along with the weighted silence, punched through Nolan's rambling thoughts and silent prayer.

Wait. What? They all looked at him. Including the legend.

"Huh?"

Ruth laughed.

Were they talking about *him*?

Just perfect. His introduction to the greatest legend in baseball, and he stood here mumbling like an idiot. His brain finally processed what had been said. That he could get one by Ruth.

Ruth rose, a grin on his lips and a challenge in his eyes. The other men started their chattering again, but Nolan couldn't make out a word of it.

A chance to pitch to *the* Babe Ruth? Who cared if he looked stupid? "Want to give it a go?"

Ruth rumbled another laugh and grabbed a bat. "Let's see what you've got."

His stomach dropped to his toes, and his gaze lurched to Pete.

Oh no.

What if he lost control with Ruth like he had with Pete?

What if he injured Babe Ruth? Would that alter history? He'd never forgive himself.

Fifteen

At least she hadn't been tossed out on her ear.
Amelia's breath came out in an uneven rush as she
stepped through Tita's door. Why did people use that
phrase, anyway? Who would land on their ear? Bottom,
shoulder, or even the head, she could see. But ear? That
seemed awfully specific. Like landing on your nose.

"To the kitchen with you." Tita jabbed a finger toward
the rear of the house.

Amelia obeyed. The kitchen seemed like as good of a
place as any to get the shakedown. Tita would either accuse
her of being crazy or bombard her with a million questions
she couldn't answer.

But at least she hadn't been thrown out on her nose.

Or ear.

Yet.

The house felt relatively cool, given the sultry temperatures outside, and Tita's domain remained spotless. Each blue or yellow tile gleamed, and the polished furniture shone. Should she take a seat at the table? That's where interrogations usually occurred, right?

But how could she explain anything about a crazy situation she didn't understand? She hardly believed it possible herself. Why would anyone else?

"Get the beef out of the icebox and then start chopping onions." Tita snagged an apron from a hook by the door and flung it around her waist.

Uh, what? "You aren't, um, aren't you going to ask me about, well, you know."

"*A trabajar primero.*"

Work first? Did that mean they would talk once they started cooking?

An odd sensation settled in Amelia's center. A mixture of familiar comfort and aching loss. Papá had been that way too. Whenever something troubled him or the family had problems to work through, they went to the kitchen.

A slow smile tugged at her lips. "*Manos ocupadas y mente despejada.*"

Busy hands and a clear mind.

Tita paused with a bag of rice in one hand. "Who told you this phrase?"

"My father." Amelia shrugged. "He used to say it all the time. Abuela did too. I think he learned it from her."

Tita mumbled something under her breath Amelia didn't quite catch. It sounded something along the lines of needing God to help her untangle the crazy.

Maybe Tita used that phrase too. Perhaps she'd been the one to pass it to her son, who passed it down the line.

Amelia almost wanted to laugh. She took the green apron tossed at her and removed two onions from the basket Tita indicated on the counter. Busy hands first. Maybe then she could clear her mind.

But honestly, an entire feast's worth of work wouldn't be enough to clear up the strange things bouncing around in her head this time.

After about ten minutes of chopping onions, garlic, and bell peppers, Tita clanged her knife to the counter. "What is this of traveling from the future? Why play tricks on me?"

"I am not playing tricks, Bisabuela." The name slipped out of its own accord, and heat rushed up her ears. Tita *was* her great-grandmother with two more greats added on, but that probably sounded inappropriate coming from a stranger. Amelia pushed past her awkwardness. "I don't know how to explain it or tell you why it has happened. I can only tell you I believe it's true. I grew up listening to stories of the brave Martita and Federico Cabrera who came to this country and built a life for the family. I know Carlo and Luis will both marry young, like their parents, and Carlo will have five sons. Luis will have two girls and then a boy. Manuel—he will be a bit different and won't settle down until one extraordinary woman catches his eye. But they will be madly in love for all their days."

Tita's mouth hung open.

"I know more, as well. But it's best not to say too much. I don't know what could change. But then, maybe it changes nothing." She turned out a palm flecked with the thin skin of a garlic clove. "I have no idea how timelines work."

Tita closed her eyes and made the symbol of the cross across her forehead and shoulders.

Maybe Amelia had said too much.

After a deep breath, Tita opened her eyes and studied Amelia as though she'd grown two ears of corn from the top of her head. Not that she could blame her.

"But how is this possible?" Tita motioned with her chin for Amelia to resume chopping tomatoes for the sauce.

Right. Busy hands to clear the mind.

She slid the knife through a green bell pepper and removed the meaty part without cutting into the seeds. "I wish I knew. I went to a bed and breakfast with my mom and—"

"Bed and breakfast? Is this like a hotel?"

Amelia slid the skin from the pepper with practiced ease. "Yes, but a private and very small one. More like an inn or *casas particulares*, a private home rented for rooms. Mamá took me there because I was sad about not getting the chef job I wanted in Atlanta."

"So you *are* a trained chef? Like the word they use for the stuffy Frenchmen?" Tita scoffed. "A woman can be such a thing in your time?"

The way she said that made Amelia think of Chef Dubois at La Petite Fleur. The man had been rather stuffy. A laugh bubbled up. "Yes, like that. There are schools specifically for professional cooks with training in how to make dishes from all over the world. Many of the students are women who will go on to have prestigious jobs as executive chefs."

Tita grinned, and the expression took years off her features. She must have been model-quality stunning in her twenties.

"This is good. Very good." Tita unwrapped a slab of beef and removed a hefty cast-iron pot from the cabinet near the stove. "Tell me more."

Where was she before they detoured onto the details of culinary school? "I didn't get the job I'd hoped for and was very upset, so Mamá wanted to do something kind for me and take me on a trip, just the two of us."

"But did you not say your father had a restaurant?"

The knife trembled in her hand. "Yes."

That wasn't the part of the statement she'd expected the other woman to latch onto. They were supposed to be discussing how she'd traveled through time. Not her failure in Atlanta.

"Then why were you not there?" Tita sprinkled cumin into the meat. "In our family's own business?"

Our family? Did that mean Tita believed her about the time travel and their relation? Before Amelia could work past the lump in her throat to answer, Tita spoke again.

"Did the restaurant close after your father moved to the next life?" She made the cross symbol again and looked up to the ceiling, though at this point Papá hadn't even been born yet.

A wrenching thought turned Amelia's knees to warm butter, and grief stung her eyes. "Why couldn't I have been sent *there*? To our restaurant, before Papá and Derick died? Why couldn't I have been set to see them again?"

The emotions came so strong and so unexpected that she dropped the knife on the cutting board and had to lean on the counter for support. She squeezed her eyes tight, and the pain leaked out in liquid form.

Warm fingers settled on her shoulder, and Tita's soft words held compassion. "Perhaps such reunions are only meant to be in heaven, where they cannot be spoiled."

Her throat still ached, but she gave a nod. How much more would it hurt to lose them again after getting them back?

Tita squeezed her shoulder and then gave Amelia a few moments to collect herself while she browned the beef. Amelia pushed the hurt back down into the deep places where she usually buried it. She finished the peppers and then seeded and chopped the rest of the tomatoes.

The familiar rhythm of cooking eased her nerves, and her heart settled even if her thoughts never did.

Once the roast browned to a perfect golden color, Tita transferred it to the pot on the stove. Next, they poured a jar of homemade beef broth over the meat, followed by the tomatoes, bell peppers, onion, garlic, cumin, cilantro, and a dash of vinegar.

"What happened to your family's restaurant after you lost your father?" Tita's gentle words pulled Amelia back into their earlier conversation.

"Mamá still keeps up with most of the finances, and we have a chef who was with us for many years." The compassion she'd felt from Tita worked like grease for her words, and they slid through her throat more easily. "But the food isn't the same, and our customers have been dwindling. We've discussed shutting the doors for good."

Tita propped a hand on her hip and pointed a wooden spoon at Amelia. "Yet here you are. A trained and professional *cocinera* without a job while your family restaurant needs a Cabrera, not some other."

"I cannot cook like my father."

Tita snorted. "Nonsense. You are just afraid."

The truth landed like a whole onion into a bowl of soup. Not only displacing the lies but also making a mess.

"I'm not afraid." Her backbone stiffened. "I planned to work in a big city. That was my goal. Just because it's different doesn't mean it's wrong."

"¡*Ja*!" Tita smothered the ropa vieja with a heavy lid and shoved it in the oven. "I know a girl trying to hide her fear with ambition when I see it."

Tita crossed her arms, pinning Amelia with a penetrating stare.

"I'm not... that's not what..." Amelia gave up the words on a huff.

Fine. Maybe it was true. "But what if I ruin everything? Destroy his legacy?"

Tita arched a brow. "You mean like by letting the restaurant he worked so hard to make a success close?"

That knifed sliced right through her heart. Mamá had said it would be okay for them to close. That her father wouldn't be disappointed in her. And he wouldn't be. She knew that. He never wanted to force his dream on her if it wasn't her dream as well. But would she be disappointed in herself if she turned her back on La Mesita?

Had she ever been as happy in any other kitchen as in the one she'd shared with her family?

"But how can I survive being in La Mesita when they are not?" Her throat tried to close over the words, but she pressed them out into the open.

"The Little Table. A perfect name for a place shared with family and friends." Tita's gentle smile belied her propensity for bluntness. "They will be there, pequeña. A bit of our ancestors' legacy is in the food we make, yes? This is how it always is for Cubanos." She shrugged. "And everyone else too, I suppose. There is love wrapped in those recipes passed from one family member to another. We remember them and honor them with the techniques passed from generation to generation. If we share the love of what we cook, we are never without those who came before us."

The sweet sentiment settled into the cracks in Amelia's heart like a rich chocolate sauce into a dry cake. Tita was right. Deep down, she'd known that, but she'd pushed it away.

She swiped a tear and attempted a rueful smile. "You are wise."

Tita waved her hand. "It comes with age. You will be a wise old abuela someday too, if that is what God sees fit." She eyed her descendant. "But then who is to say what kind of blessed life will be granted to one who got to travel through time? You did not finish explaining this."

Somehow time travel seemed to be the easier change of topic, and Amelia nodded her thanks for the switch. She needed time to think about the implications of her recent self-discovery and reflection.

She took a kitchen towel from the drawer and wiped the counter. "Mamá took me to the inn, which I should have realized might be peculiar."

"Peculiar how?"

Amelia rolled her eyes. "The woman there was totally crazy. Well, okay, not actually crazy. Just super weird. But now that I think about it, since she knew she was about to send me to the past, a lot more of what she said makes sense."

"You think this woman has magic powers to send people through time?" Tita didn't scoff, but disbelief still spiced her tone.

"No, I don't think it's magic or anything. But I think she knows it happens to people who stay in her house. She said strange things—like how I needed to go to the kitchen, but only at the right time. Once Nolan got there too." She wiggled her bottom lip through her teeth. "She said something about staying on schedule, she gave Nolan a baseball card and me a hand mixer, and then she stood back and watched us like something was about to happen."

"And what did happen?" Tita had forgotten all about busy hands now. She had both palms planted on the counter, her head cocked toward Amelia.

"I felt dizzy, and I could smell all kinds of things cooking. The next thing I knew, I was standing in the kitchen at the Breakers, and you came in minutes later."

Tita placed a hand on her forehead. "*No es de extrañar* you looked so lost."

"Yeah. No wonder at all. I'm pretty much the worst kind of lost you can be."

Tita wrapped her in a hug. "You are not lost, pequeña. You are where you need to be." She grasped Amelia's shoulders and held her back to arm's length. "And lucky for you, I know the answer to your problem."

"You do?"

"Sí." Tita clapped. "You will learn from me. I will teach you every recipe my abuela taught me and her abuela taught her. Then! Then you will go back to your time, and you will cook in your father's kitchen. You will keep your family's legacy strong. And this is where you will be happy."

Amelia stared at her.

Tita gave a firm nod. "Yes. This is the answer. Simple as that."

Amelia gripped the counter's edge until her knuckles blanched.

Right. As simple as that.

Sixteen

This was it. Sweat rolled down Nolan's neck and coated the back of his jersey. His feet shifted on the mound, sending up swirls of red dirt to cling to his pants and hang on for the show.

He couldn't do this.

Pitch to Babe Ruth, the greatest player of all time? He wasn't ready. The pressure mounted in his center and threatened to erupt from his ears.

Ruth swaggered to the batter's box and twirled a Louisville Slugger. An easy grin bunched his rounded cheeks. Did he sense even now that few would ever come close to his greatness?

Of course not. He couldn't know that. Maybe he knew he outshone his contemporaries. But standing there now, he seemed relaxed. Eager. Like the shine hadn't worn off the game and he'd turned it into nothing more than a job. Like, maybe he still loved baseball in the same way thousands of boys loved to swing a bat and spend a Saturday afternoon besting one another at the plate.

Sweat stung the corner of Nolan's eye. He swiped it away, then settled into the stretch, heartbeat pounding in his ears.

No pressure.

Only the greatest player of all time and the risk of altering history.

Right. No pressure at all.

Ruth settled his bat on his shoulder and tugged his cap. No helmets in these days. Better not hit the guy in the head.

What was he *thinking*?

Those notions had no place in his thoughts. He *would* be accurate. Had to be. Tingles raced down his arm. He held the glove to his chest. Raised his knee.

"What are you doing?" Ruth plopped the bat to the dirt and stared at him.

Nolan stuttered to a halt, his body momentum rocking him off-balance. He jarred his foot on the edge of the mound.

From the dugout, men chuckled. One let out a whistle and said something about Nolan's mental state. Which he ignored.

Mostly.

Ruth scratched his head and then strode forward. He regarded Nolan before speaking. "Where'd you learn to pitch?"

Explaining the minor leagues right now would be a stretch. But he couldn't lie either. The Brewers wouldn't exist until 1969, so he couldn't name the organization. He could go with college. Mississippi State played in the twenties. He thought so, anyway.

"Not one for many words, eh?" Ruth shrugged. "Mind if I give you a few pointers?"

"Uh...yeah."

Ruth waved him off the mound and took his place. "Set your feet forward, facing your batter. Then go like this here, see?"

He lifted both arms over his head, the ball clutched in the glove. Then he broke them apart, arms swaying down to his sides. He swung both arms all the way behind him, then up over his head again. Only then did he twist his shoulders and sink—slightly—into his hips. His knee bent, and his foot came up about six inches. Then he reared back to throw.

The ball hit the mitt with a solid *thunk*.

Interesting.

Nolan scratched his chin. He'd seen Ruth pitch before, of course. What kid with YouTube hadn't? But seeing something on video couldn't compare with real life. Strange how he'd never noticed how drastically pitching had changed over the years. And only a few days ago, he'd been thinking how baseball stayed the same.

By modern standards, Ruth's hips opened too soon, robbing him of the power of his core. He also dropped his elbow below his shoulder, which put far too much strain on his tendons. Yet he still threw hard and straight. Everything Nolan ever had drilled into him screamed of conventional mechanics, but the best pitchers all had their own style.

Hideo Nomo raised both arms straight above his head, twisted his body toward second base, and then spun around toward home to release the pitch. No one else threw like that. Yet Nomo had a successful twelve-year career in the major leagues, primarily with the Los Angeles Dodgers.

Maybe Nolan needed to focus more on what worked for him and less on what worked for someone else.

"See?" Ruth tossed the ball back to him. "You're facing your body toward third and getting twisted. Maybe that's your problem."

Nolan swallowed. "That's, um, that's how I was taught." Cool as it might be, he couldn't scrap his mechanics for a pitching motion that wouldn't hold up against modern-era hitters. At least not for him.

Ruth smacked his shoulder. "Have it your way, fella. Just trying to help."

"Yes, sir. Thank you."

"Sir?" He tipped his hat back. "It's just baseball. Don't take it so seriously."

Ruth swaggered back to the batter's box, and the other guys hanging around in the dugout and on deck elbowed one another. They'd all thought his pitching looked weird too, but they couldn't argue with his results.

Well, except for the wild pitches. And hitting Pete.

Nolan stared at the ball in his hand. What should he do now? Take advice from the greatest of all time and try to vary his mechanics, or stick with the modern-era wisdom? He ran his fingers along the thick laces of the baseball. He hadn't thrown with laces raised this much since high school. Maybe not even since junior varsity. He tossed it in the air and caught it again.

Maybe that was the problem. Raised laces gave the ball more movement. He'd been throwing like he had a major's ball when he should have been throwing like he had one for a high school league. That probably cut out the movement pitches. If he kept it simple, he'd have better control.

"Stop thinking, fella! Just throw." Ruth laughed and lifted the bat. "Give me something to hit."

Nolan grinned. Something to hit, huh? He could do that.

How long had it been since he'd had fun with the game? No worries over statics or scouts or earning playing time? No stress over getting called up to the show. He slid his fingers across the laces for a two-seam fastball.

He settled into the stretch. He could do this.

"Try setting your feet toward your batter if you want it to fly straight!" Ruth wiggled the bat.

Sorry, Babe Ruth.

Nolan needed his muscles to remember and his mind to let go. He had to find that feeling again. The sensation of the ball and the rush of adrenaline. The love of the game.

Every sandlot boy for a hundred years would give his right arm for this opportunity. He could do no less than giving it everything he had. His own way.

His body swung into his windup and he let the ball fly.

The ball screamed down the center of the plate and sank into Rufus's outstretched mitt with a force that jarred the catcher's arm.

Silence.

Nolan stared at Babe Ruth, who stared at Rufus. Then both men looked at him, Babe with wide eyes and Rufus with a wild grin.

Something warm gathered in Nolan's core. He'd just smoked one past the greatest of all time. He shook out his shoulders and took the crest of the mound again.

"I guess that's strike one!" Pete called from the dugout, breaking the strange lull hanging over the field.

The others whooped.

Ruth adjusted his hat and lifted his bat again.

Two-seamer. Right up the gut.

"Strike two!"

Rufus tossed the ball back to him, and Nolan bounced it in his hand. He could go for the curve, but why push his luck? Besides, who would ever believe he'd struck out Babe Ruth with three belt-high fastballs?

He set his feet and ignored the sweat streaking down his temples. The ball settled in his hand, the laces between his first two fingers. It felt as natural as walking. Almost an extension of him.

His body fell into the familiar rhythm. He released the ball. It rocketed through the air.

Ruth pivoted, and his bat came around.

Crack!

The ball's momentum switched in an instant as it encountered the sweet spot on the bat and then shot in the opposite direction. It soared over Nolan's head and kept rising. He turned to watch it fly past center field.

He couldn't help but laugh as he gave the ball a little wave. It kept going past the fence, over the field, and disappeared somewhere in the open land beyond.

Behind him, his temporary teammates cheered.

Ruth trotted around the bases and accepted the shoulder slaps of the other men at home plate.

Nolan's hands tingled as energy coursed through him. He'd pitched to Babe Ruth. Sure, the guy had cleared a massive homer on him, but he'd *pitched to Babe Ruth*. The little boy inside who had lived and breathed baseball did cartwheels through his head.

Ruth jogged toward the mound. "Not bad. Guess you don't need anything from me after all, huh?"

"Actually, if I run to get that ball, will you sign it for me?" Sure, he sounded like a starstruck nine-year-old with a VIP dugout pass but so what?

His inner child cheered.

Ruth laughed. "That's it, eh?"

"Well, I wouldn't object to some hitting pointers, but I think I'm happy with my pitching."

Ruth roared a belly laugh. "Good for you, fella. Good for you."

The others crowded around Ruth as Nolan hurried around the fence and sprinted to the field. Would the time-travel thing let him take home a souvenir? He had to at least try.

After searching in the tall grass, he located the ball. Authentic era too. How much would one of these be worth at home? And how would he ever explain how he'd gotten it?

A worry for later, assuming he even got to take it back with him.

Or go home at all.

He pushed the last thought aside. He didn't think God would strand him in the past. Mrs. Easley's letter said they had to come to learn something. He grabbed the ball and tossed it up, then palmed the leather.

He'd learned plenty. He'd learned he needed to remember to have fun with the game. He could do his best. But if and when he got called to the majors wouldn't be on his timeline, and other than giving it his all, he had no control over the matter.

And he owed his dad an apology for staying away because he'd feared his family had been disappointed in him when they'd never given him any indication to validate those insecurities.

Plenty of life-lesson learning right there. But then there was also Amelia. He'd pointed out how she avoided risk, but he'd done the same. He'd been too afraid to jump into anything with the one woman who never strayed far from his thoughts. He'd feared rejection or that somehow he'd be dishonoring his best friend.

As he jogged around the fence to join the others, peace settled on him. As soon as he got home, he'd do things differently. And once he finished here, he'd head straight to the Cabrera house and ask Amelia to make things between them official.

The men parted, and Nolan held the ball out to Ruth. "Got a pen?"

None of them did. After a bit of searching, Bobby found one with the manager's notes in the locker room. Nolan tossed the ball to Ruth and watched as he scrawled his name on the side.

"Hey, can I get one of those too?" Pete leaned over Ruth's shoulder.

"Sure." Ruth smirked. "Soon as you throw me one I can hit out of the park."

The men all laughed, and Ruth held out the ball worth at least ten grand in Nolan's time.

His palms slicked as he reached for it. "Thank you. It was an honor to pitch to you, sir."

"Sir again, eh?"

Nolan's fingers brushed the stitched leather, and a wave of heat enveloped him. What in the...?

"None of that now." Ruth chuckled. "You just keep doing what you're doing, and you might be pitching for the Yankees someday."

The Yankees?

Nolan's head swam. Why did he feel so dizzy...?

He gripped the ball tight as the voices around him faded.

Then everything went black.

Seventeen

Tita had been wrong. Amelia stirred a chocolate sauce in the hotel kitchen as the sun sprinkled its first rays of light through the upper windows. They'd spent hours yesterday going over every recipe Amelia could remember from her family's cookbook.

Yet she'd woken up this morning, still stuck in the past.

Though, to be honest, she hadn't been as upset by the revelation as she should've been. What would more time hurt? Nolan wanted to stay until Saturday to see Babe Ruth play. Fine with her. That gave her one more night with Tita to learn.

Tita had even told Amelia stories of her own grand-mother, who had perfected many of their treasured flavor combinations. They'd worked and talked and laughed well into the night.

She lifted the spoon and checked the sauce's consistency. Perfect.

The time in her abuela's kitchen had been so...satisfying. Almost as though her heart had been longing for something to fill in the cracks grief had left behind, but she hadn't known how. When she got home, she would need to get Mamá in the kitchen again. Papá and Derick might be gone, but the two Cabrera women could honor their memory together.

In her grief, she'd pushed every reminder of her father and brother away when what she'd needed was to pull them closer.

"As long as we share the love of what we cook, we are never without those who came before us." Tita's words replayed in her head as she stirred sauce that didn't need more mixing.

One evening with Tita hadn't given her any major revelations, and she still didn't know how she felt about stepping into a job at La Mesita. But she didn't have to know all the answers right now. She had time to figure things out.

Too bad Nolan hadn't come for supper at Rico and Tita's last night. She had so much to tell him. But her lack of invitation and his team practice must've kept him away. Poor Nolan. Caught up in learning family recipes, she'd neglected him. Her stomach pitched. She'd check on him as soon as she got a break.

She tested the sauce. Creamy and delicious. Now, what else had Tita told her to start on this morning? They were making French toast and chocolate sauce, pancakes, a fruit medley, and muffins with fresh blueberry jam.

Movement drew her eye to the doorway, and her heart lurched at the sight of a porter's uniform. The skinny man with a shock of wheat-colored hair, however, wasn't the one who made her pulse rocket.

Pete, who showed no signs of his bruised ribs, sauntered into the kitchen and lingered by the doorway, his gaze bouncing around the room.

He could take a message to Nolan. Having to wait to tell someone something had never been an inconvenience she'd had to deal with, and she wouldn't take text messages for granted again.

When she caught Pete's eye, she waved the young baseball player over. He sidled up to her as she placed a cutting board on the counter.

"Good morning. Would you mind giving Nolan a message when you see him?" She rested a paring knife on the cutting board for the strawberries. The recipe didn't call for them, but one never went wrong adding fresh-chopped strawberries to chocolate sauce.

"Can't. He's gone." Pete smoothed a hand over his goopy hair, gaze darting to the stove to his left.

Amelia plunked her spoon onto the counter, sending flecks of chocolate sauce all over the surface. "What do you mean Nolan's gone?"

Pete shrugged, his restless gaze bouncing to Edna, who hadn't yet looked up from the blueberry jam she had been stirring for the last ten minutes. "We all think maybe he went with Ruth. Georgie did say he might play for the Yankees someday, and ain't none of us seen him since the two of them was talking yesterday."

He fiddled with the collar of his red uniform jacket and bounced on his toes.

Amelia snapped her fingers to regain Pete's attention. Bangs flopped across his forehead as he jerked his head her way. "Who is going to play for the Yankees? Babe Ruth?"

"Don't you keep up? He was already traded. He's a Yankee now already."

"Yes, but he's not supposed to be here yet." A pounding started behind her right eye. That had been the thing, right? Babe Ruth would come on Saturday. Nolan would see the legend play, and then they would go home. Why was he here on Friday? "And what does Babe Ruth playing for the Yankees have to do with Nolan?"

"Not Ruth. Ruth already plays for the Yankees." Pete scooped a glob of chocolate from the counter and examined it on the end of his finger. "I mean that Ruth told Nolan he might be able to play for the Yankees. Then he hit a four-bagger way out over the fence. Ruth, not Nolan, of course. Nolan got the ball signed, which was lucky for him, seeing as how we all know Ruth is going to be one of the greats. Might even end up as good as Ty Cobb. Course, Cobb is a fielder, and Ruth is a pitcher with a good bat. Then there's all them rumors about Cobb, but that don't mean much for his game."

"Pete!" Amelia groaned. "That's not important. What happened to Nolan?"

He stuck his finger in his mouth and licked off the chocolate sauce. "Nothing happened to him. He probably just ran off with Ruth to see if he could play for the Yankees like Ruth said."

Ice formed in her center. Nolan wouldn't have run off. But what if meeting Babe Ruth had triggered his time travel? A Babe Ruth baseball card had sent Nolan here. Would a signed baseball send him home?

She slicked damp palms down her apron. "I need to go find him."

Pete eyed another dollop of chocolate on the counter.

"Better not let Tita see you do that." Amelia grabbed a rag and cleaned the mess, then deposited the bowl of sauce out of Pete's reach.

"Did he say anything to you about Edna?" Pete's words stopped her progress untying her apron.

"What do you mean?"

He shoved his hands in his pockets. "Just with the way she was looking at him. I wondered, since you two are friends and all, if he said anything about her. Like if he was thinking about sharing a soda or something with her."

Amelia rolled her eyes. "Nolan isn't interested in your girl. Besides, she was just being nice to him earlier. Doesn't mean she doesn't like you."

His eyes brightened. "Did she say that?"

Amelia didn't know the first thing about the girl's love interests, and she didn't have time to play matchmaker. "Why don't you go ask her yourself? Girls like that, you know. A man with confidence."

The challenge inflated Pete's chest, and he cleaned his hands on his pants before striding Edna's way. If Tita caught him flirting with one of the girls in her kitchen, he wouldn't last fifteen seconds.

Amelia should find her ancestor before abandoning her job, but she needed to assuage the dread churning in her stomach. If Ruth came early and saw Nolan without her, did that mean Nolan got sent home and she didn't?

She located Rico and Tita in the garden. They were holding an animated conversation in Spanish. Rico noticed her over Tita's shoulder and switched to English.

"We were just talking about you. Seems you have some tall tales for mi corazón." His tone carried equal parts censure and humor.

"Nolan is missing. I came to tell you I need to go look for him."

"Missing?" Tita placed her hand on her collar. "Do you think he went back to the future without you?"

Hearing her fears spoken aloud increased the ball of ice in her gut. "I'm too distracted worrying about that to be any good in the kitchen. I need to go find out."

Rico gripped his wife's shoulder and leveled a heavy gaze at Amelia. "Why are you saying these things? Telling my wife that you are our descendant? This cannot be, as you are standing here now. What trick is this?"

Amelia rubbed the place between her thumb and forefinger to release the tension headache gathering steam. "It isn't a trick. I've been nothing but honest with the both of you, even if the truth seems impossible."

Rico grunted. "It is best if you find your own lodging now, yes? This is too much."

No. She couldn't. She needed to have the lessons and...

All her protests died in her throat before she could voice them. Who could blame him? She would think the same in his position.

"I must teach her, love. It is important." Tita's compassion knotted Amelia's heart.

"You are giving away secrets meant only for family. I thought you would never do this thing." Rico shook his head. "It is a trick. She will take your abuela's secrets for her own use."

Tita lifted her chin. "They are my abuela's secrets, and I will share them if I want to. Besides, I believe her. She must save Manuel's restaurant."

"Manuel has a restaurant?" Rico wrinkled his nose. "He cannot cook a boiled egg."

Tita huffed. "His great-grandson will be a successful man who owns his own restaurant, and he will believe in his *hija*. He will leave his legacy to her. A woman who will be a famous cocinera."

Amelia didn't know about being a famous chef, but Tita's easy confidence that Papá had believed in her—and that he would leave his legacy to her—bolstered her heart. She straightened her shoulders. "I'm not lying, señor. I am the daughter of Manuel, who is the descendant of your youngest son. I have heard the stories all my life. It was my great privilege to meet you and Tita. You are an inspiration to our family. Your names are honored for generations."

Rico's eyes misted. He shook his head again but still managed a slight smile. "I cannot believe what you say is true, but it is my hope that someday my children and their children's children will believe these things about us."

She turned to Tita. "Thank you for all you've taught me. If you think of any more recipes to add to the book, I'll have them when I get home." A laugh bubbled free. "Just maybe try to add in more precise measurements this time, okay? It will make it easier for us to remember if you use things like teaspoons instead of 'a little bit' and rather than 'until it tastes right,' maybe something more definitive."

Tita grinned. "That was how it was taught to me, so it's how I write it down."

"Yes, but we don't have you to teach us, and some of these things are lost over the years. I didn't know until you showed me because we couldn't replicate the recipes without measurements. 'A little bit' to me was not the same as a little bit to those before me, and I did not know what 'tasted right' before I had eaten yours. How will I pass the dishes to my daughters if I don't know how to make them properly?"

"*Estás en lo correcto.* You are correct. I will write down the technique as well as the measurements." She slid free of Rico's grasp and gathered Amelia into a hug. "You are a good girl. Do not let fear hold you back."

Amelia swallowed the lump in her throat. "I'll try."

Tita stepped back to look her in the eyes, one hand rising to smooth Amelia's hair. "No. You will promise." Tita patted Amelia's cheek. "Life is hard enough, pequeña. You must be brave and willing to fight for your dreams. If you do not, you might end up an old woman in a rocking chair in Cuba instead of one in a tiny house in Florida, yes?"

She smiled. If Rico and Tita hadn't taken risks, then they would have never come to America. How might that have changed their family's history? How might her decisions affect the generations after her?

"I promise. Thank you, Bisabuela."

She gave Tita one last hug, waved to Rico, and set off to find the man she hoped to start building that future with.

Eighteen

What was she going to do now? Tears Amelia refused to let fall burned her eyes as she trudged down the sidewalk to Tita's house. No sign of Nolan anywhere. Pitying expressions and patronizing words came from every person she'd asked.

They all seemed to think he'd abandoned her. Took off with Babe Ruth and went to play for the Yankees. She'd asked every porter and employee she could find.

Nolan was gone.

Obviously, not with the 1920 Yankees. Not that she could explain *that* to anyone.

Why would Nolan be sent home while she remained behind? She'd started to think their relationship had been one of those "lessons" Mrs. Easley said they had to learn in

181

order to go home. But how could that be if he left and she didn't? It took two people for a relationship, after all.

She blew out a breath and forced her feet forward over the bridge. Was she going to be stuck in the past, homeless and alone? Not alone, sure. Rico and Tita would take her in, even if Rico did think she could be crazy. Kindness ran too deep in both.

What was she missing?

She'd accepted she needed to take a few risks. Starting with Nolan. She'd confronted buried hurts about her father and brother. She'd learned family cooking secrets. But here she remained, standing outside of her great-great-great-grandparents' house with nothing more than an outlandish story and a confused heart. She'd never felt so out of control.

Her fist hesitated over the door.

Just knock.

A moment later, Rico opened the door. His eyebrows climbed toward graying brown hair. "Buenas noches."

"Good evening." She shifted her feet.

He didn't open the door or invite her in. Maybe she'd been wrong, and he wouldn't let her stay after all. What would happen to her if she didn't have distant family to help her?

Memories of all those times Mamá had tried to offer help, but Amelia had pushed her away surfaced. Her pride said she was independent and capable. That she didn't need help from anyone.

Trouble was that a woman could be both independent and accept loving help when offered. Maybe that had been part of what she still needed to learn.

She clicked her heels together, just in case.

Nothing happened. Well, other than Rico staring at her like she'd grown two heads. Guess her plain black pumps didn't work as ruby-red slippers.

Swallowing some of her pride now, Amelia summoned a tired smile. "I am sorry to bother you, señor. But, well, I was wondering if..."

He widened the door. "If you could stay in our home until a time machine takes you to the future?"

Time machine?

He chuckled at the confusion surely on her face. "I have read this book, *The Time Machine*, by Mr. Wells. I do not know why you also tell such fantasies or how you convinced my wife they are true, but she believes you. Me, not so much. But I do believe you are a good Christian girl who needs help." He waved his hand for her to enter. "So, we will let you stay."

Air leaked out of her. "Thank you."

She followed him to the kitchen where Tita chopped plantains. The older woman dropped the knife as soon as she spotted Amelia.

"Oh! You are still here." She wiped her hands on a rag. "Come, I have thought of another dish we must make. *Lo siento*. I should have thought of it sooner. It is the most important."

Amelia grabbed an apron as Tita piled apples on the counter.

"I got the ingredients this afternoon, in case you came back." Tita polished one of the apples on her apron. "This was *bisabuela's* favorite." She snapped her fingers and pointed to a notebook Amelia recognized. "I do not know why I didn't include it in the book, but it is there now."

That was her father's recipe book. The one that had been her grandmother's and her grandmother's before her. Now Tita had included her own great-grandmother's recipes in it. How many generations did that make? Amelia counted back. Tita's bisabuela would be Amelia's fifth great-grandmother.

Seven generations.

"Chop those. Then put them in that pot." Tita nodded to the stove, tugging Amelia from counting ancestors.

She did as instructed while Tita laid out the other ingredients.

"Three-fourths of a cup of piloncillo." Tita placed a compact cone of rich cane sugar on the counter. "Or cut this about here. Then one tablespoon of lemon juice, one teaspoon of vanilla, one-fourth teaspoon of ground cinnamon, and one-eighth teaspoon of these ground cloves."

Rico chuckled as he plopped into a kitchen chair. "She spent all afternoon measuring and writing. Usually, she makes these by memory." He patted his stomach. "Not that I minded eating her test batch, of course."

They shared a laugh as Amelia settled into chopping the apples and adding them to the pan followed by the rest of the ingredients Tita had named. While the apples simmered, releasing a mouthwatering aroma, they began the flaky crust for the empanadas.

Flour, sugar, salt, and two sticks of cold butter cut into pieces were laid out on the work surface.

"Now, this is important." Tita notched a hand on her hip. "You use the turbinado for the dust on the outside. This is the secret." She shifted a few grains of the minimally processed sugar cane.

Amelia set the flour, regular white sugar, and salt into a bowl and used Tita's hand mixer to blend the ingredients.

Next, she cut in the butter, two eggs, and two tablespoons of water while Tita supervised over her shoulder.

Once the dough formed, they rolled it onto a floured surface and kneaded it into a ball.

"Now we cut it into four pieces." Tita sliced the ball one way and then the other. "Then again."

Sixteen hunks of dough waited on the table. Amelia eyed Rico. Had he eaten all sixteen empanadas from the last batch?

"Roll out each piece into a nice ball with the palm of your hand." Tita demonstrated with the first lump and then motioned for Amelia to do the same.

The tantalizing scent of the apples on the stove made her mouth water as they used a wooden roller to flatten the balls into six-inch disks. Then they placed those onto parchment paper and tucked them into the icebox to cool.

"Tita, can I ask you something?" Amelia wiped her hands on a rag, avoiding eye contact.

The other woman paused stirring the apples. "Anytime."

"Can I stay here if I can't go home?"

"Of course." Rico snorted from behind the newspaper covering his face. "We will not turn out anyone who can make apple empanadas. And any of my other favorite desserts on the days when mi corazón will not make them for me."

Tita waved a yellow towel his way. "Ignore him. Of course you can stay. But I think you will go home. As soon as you learn this recipe."

That's what she'd said about the six others they'd worked on yesterday. Whatever Amelia needed to learn would take more time. Well, time she had in abundance.

I trust your timing, God. Help me to learn what I need to learn.

Peace settled within her even as her stomach growled. She'd missed supper.

Tita fed her leftover rice and beans while they waited for the apples to soften and then cool and the dough to chill.

After Amelia finished, they filled each circle with apples, folded over one edge, and pinched the sides together. Tita sliced a little *X* into the top of each, brushed them with egg whites, and sprinkled turbinado sugar on the tops before the delicacies went into the oven to bake.

Thirty minutes later, Tita displayed the warm pastries on the table. Amelia handed out three chipped plates and joined her elders. The inviting scents of apple and cinnamon tempted her taste buds. She blew on an empanada to cool it, then bit into it.

Sweetness erupted on her tongue, and she closed her eyes. "Mmm. These are much better than the ones we make."

Tita grinned. "See? This is what you needed." She tested a corner and smiled at Rico.

He stared at Amelia, but when she didn't disappear into thin air, he shrugged and snagged an empanada. Half of it vanished in one bite.

She let herself eat three more before her stomach protested.

"I'll help you clean the kitchen." She pushed her chair under the table. "Thank you for these, Tita. They are spectacular."

"Good enough for La Mesita?" She wiggled her eyebrows.

"*Por supuesto*. We will call them Bisabuela Tita's delights."

That gained a laugh from both Tita and Rico.

"You have decided, then? You will go home to your father's restaurant?" Tita draped her apron over the back of the chair and smoothed the edges.

"I think so, yes. It's where I always belonged."

Tita clapped. "*Perfecto*! This is good." She waved toward the mess they'd left in the kitchen. "Now, to work."

This time Amelia didn't need the busy hands to allow her mind to clear. For the first time in a long while, she knew the next steps she wanted to take.

She gathered the measuring spoons, dropped them into a bowl, and wiped flour from the counter. Then she grabbed the hand mixer to add it to the bowl so she could carry everything to the sink in one trip.

Wait. Didn't the mixer she'd used earlier have a black handle? This one was painted red.

Just like...

Her head swam as a dizziness rushed over her. She gripped the counter. "Tita? I think..." The breathy words died on her lips.

Then everything went black.

Nineteen

Nolan blinked and stared at the card in his hand. How long had he been sitting here? He shook his head, trying to dispel the fog. Was that Mrs. Easley smiling at him?

"What did you think of George?"

Something about the way she asked the question said they both knew she didn't refer to the baseball card.

He dropped it on the kitchen counter. "Where's Amelia?"

Mrs. Easley smoothed an apron over a simple blouse and flatted a ball of dough with a rolling pin. When had she changed clothes? Had he been gone a couple of days or the blink of an eye?

"She'll be back soon. No need to worry."

He popped from the stool, and pain lanced through his arm. He winced. He'd forgotten about that in the—days? minutes?—he'd been gone.

"Why don't you take it easy, hmm?" Mrs. Easley didn't look up.

Easy. Yeah, maybe he should. Why did his head feel like the inside of an old baseball? Stuffed with yarn. His mind worked to unravel the tangle of questions vying for position. He settled on the one that mattered most.

"What did you do with Amelia?"

Mrs. Easley set the dough on parchment paper with three others and fingered another lump, working it into a perfect ball. "I haven't done anything with her, and as I said, she will return shortly. How about you answer my question while we wait? What did you think of George?"

His gaze snagged on the baseball card on the counter. He didn't dare touch it. "I had an autographed ball. Ruth signed it."

That sounded crazy.

Still, he patted his pockets. Empty. His heart dropped. Oh well. He should have known he wouldn't get to keep it. Talk about something hard to explain. Not that he'd be selling it or anything.

Mrs. Easley offered a sad smile. "We can't always bring things back with us. Sometimes it's allowed. Other times, it's not in the plan."

Would have been cool to have some kind of proof he'd traveled to the past. That had been what had happened, right? Or had he been sitting here daydreaming, and Amelia got bored and left him to his fantasies?

No, that couldn't be. Too much had happened for it to have been concocted in his head. He cleared his throat. "Why did you want me to meet Babe Ruth?"

She cut him a glance before stacking her next tiny pizza-crust-looking thing on the tray with the others. "Wasn't my idea, young man. The Conductor sends his children where they need to go to see who they need to see. I've never met George myself, but my dear husband was a big fan." She nodded to the card, which must have belonged to Mr. Easley. "It's merely curiosity behind my question."

He let that settle. She'd put a heavy emphasis on the word *Conductor*. What did that mean? No telling with this woman. At least she didn't pretend she hadn't shoved him into the past. By Conductor, did she mean God?

What did that mean about Mrs. Easley and the kind of access she had to the Creator? Nope. Nolan mentally shook his head. Too much for his brain to hold. He focused on doing as she asked instead of trying to unwind mysteries too great for him. He'd have to trust that God had given him what he needed. Nothing more, nothing less.

He let out a long breath. "Babe Ruth was a lot like I expected him to be. Confident, crazy talented, and friendly. He signed the home-run ball he hit off me." A laugh lurched from his throat. "Can you imagine that? Me. Pitching to the Great Bambino."

Mrs. Easley wiped her hands on her apron before grabbing another ball of dough. How many miniature pizzas did she need to make? "From what I understand, you're a pretty good ballplayer yourself. You just needed someone you could believe to tell you."

Babe Ruth had been someone he could believe?

He'd been told he could play ball better than most since the third grade. Coaches, teachers, friends, and his parents had all poured into him. Had he never believed it himself until Babe Ruth said he could play for the Yankees?

Why? Had he doubted himself and those around him that much?

"Sometimes we let ourselves overthink, yes? What do you children call it? Getting in your head." Mrs. Easley stuck the tray in the refrigerator and checked her watch. "Any moment now."

Before he could ask what she meant by that, Mrs. Cabrera swept into the room. "Nolan! So good to see you."

"Hey, Miss Sarah. How are you?" He rose to greet her with a hug.

She patted the shoulder on his good arm. "I'm fine. What about you? Your mother told me you are going to be out for several weeks. I'm so sorry."

The sympathy in her tone didn't sting like it would've before his time in the past. "It's okay. I need time to refocus anyway."

A tinkle of laughter came from across the room. They both turned to look at Mrs. Easley, who wore a satisfied grin. "Oh, never mind me. I'm always pleased as punch when things turn out."

Mrs. Cabrera shot a questioning look at Nolan, who could only shake his head.

"Where's Amelia?" Mrs. Cabrera slid her gaze over the mess Mrs. Easley had made in the kitchen. "I thought you two were going on a date."

"She'll be back in a moment." The older woman waved them toward the door. "Why don't you two take some lemonade to the parlor to wait?"

Probably a good idea. Mrs. Cabrera would be in for a shock if her daughter materialized out of thin air. Assuming that's how it worked. He had no idea. He'd returned to the same position he'd been in when he'd left, so it stood to reason the same would happen for Amelia.

Mrs. Cabrera accepted the two glasses of ice while Nolan took the pitcher of lemonade. Soon, the two of them settled into Victorian-style furniture in the front room.

"Where did she say Amelia went?" Mrs. Cabrera perched on a low couch covered in floral fabric.

Not wanting to lie, Nolan shrugged. He set the pitcher on a short table before lowering himself into a dainty chair. The furniture here wasn't meant for men his size.

"Perhaps she slipped off to take a moment to gather herself." Mrs. Cabrera poured both glasses for them and then without sampling any placed her drink on a coaster on the end table. "She's pretty nervous."

"About what?" No way Amelia could have known they'd be going to the past. And her mother couldn't mean seeing him made her nervous. They'd been friends for far too long for that. He sipped the tangy liquid. Perfect balance of sweet and tart.

Mrs. Cabrera lifted an eyebrow in the same "really?" expression her daughter used. "You know today marks a change in things. For some reason, she's always thought she'd be upsetting her brother if she dated you. Though to tell you the truth, she's had her heart set on you since she was fifteen."

A far-off look glazed her blue eyes. "I think that's why she never went out with many guys. Being too focused on her career was an excuse." Mrs. Cabrera drew back, pursed her lips, then eyed him like he'd been the one to spill the beans. "¡*Ay*! She won't be happy I told you that."

He chuckled. Hearing her mother confirm Amelia had always reciprocated feelings he'd harbored himself loosened a tightness in his chest. "I've always cared for Amelia. But as my best friend's little sister..." He let the admission dangle.

"She was off-limits?" Mrs. Cabrera finished for him.

"Yeah." He rubbed the back of his neck. "But I don't want to waste any more time."

She smiled and opened her mouth to say something, but truth burst out of Nolan before he could stop himself.

"I love her. I have always loved her, I think. And I'm no longer afraid to admit it. I want to build a future with her."

Mrs. Cabrera smacked her hands together. "Finally!" She grinned. "I've known it all along. Manuel and I used to say all the time that someday you two would end up together." A sad smile curved her lips. "He would have given you his blessing, you know. As Derick would have. You've always been a part of this family."

Emotion welled inside him, and he could only trust himself to give a nod of thanks.

"A bit of advice, though?"

"I'd be happy with any you have to offer."

"Amelia has been struggling. She's trying to find her place in the world, and losing Manuel and Derick has made it much harder for her. She's afraid to risk because she's afraid to fail. I think because the pain of failure is more than she can add to the pain of loss. That's why when it didn't work out in Atlanta, it nearly crushed her."

"I would never purposely hurt her. I'll do my best to help her in any way I can."

Mrs. Cabrera patted his hand. "I believe you. My advice runs in a different direction. When all that hurt overflows, she responds by pulling away. If you care for her, then try to be patient with her. Be there for her even when she pushes you away. Because that's when she needs you close the most."

"Yes, ma'am. I will."

"You're a good man, Nolan." She brushed a tear from the corner of her eye. "I'm thankful to have you in our lives."

"Same." The single word fell short, but his expression must've shown his earnestness because she smiled.

She rose and took her lemonade. "I'll go up to our room and check on Amelia. I'll send her down if I find her up there fretting."

She wouldn't find Amelia up there, but he thanked her and let her draw their conversation to a close.

While he waited, he fished his phone from his pocket and tapped the first contact.

Dad answered on the fourth ring. "Nolan! How was your date?"

Leave it to Dad to jump straight in. "Haven't been on it yet. I'm waiting on her now."

"Then what are you doing calling me?" The humor belied the words, though they still held curiosity.

"I called to apologize. Today, I realized I've put a barrier between us because I feared you'd be disappointed in me. But that wasn't fair. You and Mom have never been anything but supportive."

Seconds of silence ticked by, and Nolan tensed.

When his dad spoke, emotion clouded his voice. "We've always been proud of you, son. I don't want you to ever doubt that. No matter what path God takes you on, we are always proud you are our son."

"I know, Dad. Thank you." He cleared his throat. "So, I was thinking I'd spend my recovery time at home with you and Mom, if that's okay."

"We'd love nothing better."

They chatted about regular things, then said their good-byes with Nolan's promise to call later tonight and let them know how his date with Amelia turned out. If things went as he hoped, there'd be plenty to tell.

He stuffed his phone into his pocket and leaned back onto the cushion, more at peace than he'd ever remembered.

Thanks for the trip, Lord. Help me to remember all the lessons once life goes back to normal.

He drew a deep breath and headed toward the kitchen. Only one thing left to do.

Offer his heart to a feisty chef.

Twenty

Amelia dropped the mixer to the floor. One belonging not to a cozy bungalow in Florida, but to a time-warping Victorian B&B in Mississippi.

"Oh good. There you are." Mrs. Easley clattered something onto the counter. "You promised to help with my recipe, remember?"

Amelia swallowed and tried to collect her thoughts. She still smelled Tita's apple empanadas. Had her nose carried the smells with her?

No, a pot of the apples simmered on the stove. On the counter, a tray of empanada crusts waited. She met Mrs. Easley's gaze. "What did you do?"

"I followed the recipe, but I can't help but think something is missing. It's lacking a certain"—she snapped her fingers—"flair. Yes, that's it. Something to give it that extra touch."

Amelia gripped the counter. "You sent me to the past. And Nolan." Her heart tripped. "Where is Nolan?"

He had gone home before her, right?

"Don't panic, dear. He's in the parlor having a much-needed conversation with his father. Why don't you give him a moment and help me with this recipe."

"You sent me to the past." She repeated the sentence the older woman hadn't responded to. "I went to 1920, and you sent me there."

Mrs. Easley smiled. "Welcome to the Depot dear, where you can step back 'inn' time and leave your trouble behind."

"So you admit it!" The words squeaked out of her tight throat. "Why did you do that to me?"

"I am not the Conductor, young lady." She leveled a grandmotherly look of admonishment at Amelia that almost immediately melted. "Do you regret your time away?"

Well, no. Still. She crossed her arms in childish defiance, then deflated. "I enjoyed getting to meet Tita and Rico. I learned a lot. She even said..." The words trailed off as she remembered the recipe book.

Mrs. Easley nodded behind her. "Over there, dear."

"You've been using my bisabuela's recipe book?"

"Of course not. That would be impolite without asking your permission first. Besides, if I had done that, I wouldn't need you to help me with my own recipe, now would I?"

Amelia ignored the woman and snagged the worn leather book from the counter. She ran a finger over the embossed flower on the front and then eased open the cover. Her throat caught as she saw the first page.

Pequeña,

Here are the beloved foods of our family. Each time you make them, remember those who came before you. Let their love flavor every dish you prepare. Let their traditions become your own and pass them down to the next generation. Allow your ancestors' legacy to give you strength as you forge your own. When your mind is cluttered, keep your hands busy. Thank the God of time and family for all your blessings and remember that our love stays with you always.

Tita

Amelia held the book to her heart and let out a long breath. The generations before her would have all benefited from Tita's words, but they were meant for her. Tita had believed her. What had they thought when she disappeared from their kitchen?

She smiled to herself. Tita probably swatted Rico with a rag, and he'd had to admit she'd been right all along. Then he probably finished off the last of the apple empanadas while mumbling something about time machines and having no one to make him treats whenever Tita was mad at him.

Thumbing through the pages, she found more recipes than had been in there before, further proof she'd spent time in the past. And along with the ingredients—with proper measurements this time—came detailed instructions for the "old way" techniques. Ways, Tita claimed, made the dish more authentic.

Amelia laughed over one note, reading it aloud. "'Modern technology might give you ways to make shortcuts, but don't be fooled. Faster is not always better. Food, like hearts, needs time to develop. Don't rush either.'"

Mrs. Easley grinned. "Your ancestor sounds like a wise woman."

"She was." Amelia set the book down as an ache pinched her heart. Another person she had lost. She'd never see Rico and Tita again this side of heaven.

But then, if she hadn't been on this adventure, she never would've met them in the first place. Maybe there was truth in that trite old saying after all. Better to have loved and lost than never to have loved at all.

Pain came with love, but that didn't mean it wasn't worth it.

The thought reminded her of Nolan, and her gaze lingered on the baseball card still on the table.

No more holding back.

She resisted the urge to run to him, as he had lessons of his own to tend to. But as soon as he came back, she'd let him know she would no longer fear the risk. She loved him, and he needed to know almost as much as she needed to tell him.

To keep her hands busy as Tita instructed, Amelia flung an apron around her going-out dress and leaned down to smell Mrs. Easley's empanada filling. "Did you use piloncillo in the filling? And you'll need turbinado to the dust on the outside. That's the secret."

"Well, what a coincidence. I found some of that at a lovely Latin market just this morning. Who knew it would come in handy today?"

Amelia's lips parted as she stared at the older woman. Coincidence her foot.

Instead of pointing out the obvious, she stirred Mrs. Easley's apples. "Give them more time to soften." She breathed in the aroma. "And you need more cloves."

"Thank you, dear." A second later, she clapped her hands. "Oh! Time's up."

What?

Amelia turned to find Nolan standing in the doorway, staring at her. His arm rested in the sling, and he wore the same button-up shirt he'd come in for their date. That had been days ago, in a way.

She dropped the spoon in the pan and launched herself into his good arm. "I've missed you!"

His warm breath tickled the top of her head. "I've only been gone a few minutes, right?"

She ignored his teasing and snuggled into the warmth of his side. Being here with Nolan felt right.

"If you'll keep an eye on my apples for me, I do believe I need to—well, I'm sure there's something I need to attend to somewhere else."

Neither of them glanced at Mrs. Easley as she slipped out of the kitchen.

Nolan's gaze captured Amelia's. "I don't want to hold back anymore. I know it's sudden in a lot of ways, but I love you. I want to be with you."

Her heart pounded against her ribs. "I don't want to hold back either. I love you too."

He lowered his lips to hers, and their sweet caress loosened something within her.

Too soon, he drew back. "Will you go on a date with me?"

"Yes." Hadn't they established that already?

He kissed her again, this time cupping her cheek and drawing her closer. "Will you be my girlfriend?"

She smiled underneath the tenderness of his lips. "We haven't gone on a real date yet, but yes."

He straightened to his considerable height after pecking a kiss on her forehead. "I'm trying to go through all the steps here, Miss Cabrera, if you'll kindly let me."

"Oh. Of course, sir. Do continue." She giggled, a carefree sound that hadn't bubbled out of her in a long time.

"Will you be my longtime serious girlfriend, the kind I know I can take to weddings and that kind of thing?"

She ran her fingers through his hair. Apparently, he considered that the next step after a regular girlfriend. She let teasing slip into her tone. "I suppose that might be all right."

He spent longer kissing her then, and she melted into him.

"One more question." His voice lowered, carrying the weight of meaning.

Her pulse thrummed. Only one thing came after the kind of girlfriend you took to weddings. Words blurted out of her before she could stop them. "I'm going to keep my father's restaurant."

He blinked, then rubbed a thumb along her cheek. "Perfect. I think you should."

"You'll get called up one day. I know you will." She placed a tiny kiss on his lips to keep him from speaking yet. "What happens if I need to stay home in Brandon, and you have to go to Milwaukee?"

He pecked the end of her nose with a chaste kiss. "Life has lots of questions we can't know the answers to. We don't know what might happen with my baseball career."

She started to protest that of course he would play, but he silenced her in the same way she'd done to him. His lips felt too nice to not yield to the distraction.

Nolan drew away from her, his expression serious. "I'm going to spend some time at home with my parents while my elbow heals. After that, we'll see how the season goes and what my next one will look like. But I don't want to waste any time with what-ifs or base my most important decisions on scenarios that have no guarantee."

He had a point. What if La Mesita couldn't be saved? What if she'd need to take her family's recipes and Papá's legacy somewhere new? They had no idea what the future might hold. Why put off being with Nolan now by worrying over what situations might happen later?

"You're right. Whatever comes, we'll make those decisions together." She put her hand around his neck and drew him close. "Now, what else were you going to ask me?"

A smile curved his lips. "How about we have our lunch as a first date and then go for a nice dinner date for our second? Then we can stop at a jewelry store and make it official?"

Rather than answering, she pressed his lips to hers and let the rest of the world fade away.

Somewhere in the background, the scent of scorched apples tingled her awareness, but she pushed it away.

She, Nolan, and Mamá would make a new batch for Mrs. Easley later.

To celebrate the engagement.

Epilogue

Mrs. Easley settled into her favorite library chair to see who the Conductor might send her way next. Three days had passed since the lovely chef and her ballplayer had celebrated their engagement with festivities in her kitchen. Such days were additional blessings to the job she enjoyed. She'd wished the happy couple well and sent them on their way.

After they'd checked out, she'd had a couple of days to herself. An irregular occurrence, but the quiet time to rest on her own had been nice.

But now it was time to see who would join her next. Perhaps there would be several since the house currently stood empty. She flipped open the pages to today's date.

"Oh my!" She leaned away from the heavy tome on her desk and waved a lace fan across her face. "In all my years, this has never happened. Are you sure?"

She read over the page again, but the entry hadn't changed.

"How will this even work? It's never been done."

Peace flowed through her. Right. The Conductor had a plan. He always did. But...this?

She bounded from her seat. This would need to be an extended stay. She dropped the fan on the desk and paced the library. What about other guests? They would cause an additional challenge.

There would already be so much to do! Any other guests could prove too much of a shock. This gal must be exceptional if the Conductor thought she could handle such a transition.

She checked the book, and air slid out of her in a rush. Good. No other adventures were planned for this week. That would give her the time and devoted attention this one would require.

She twisted her watch into view. Best hurry. Would it be one room or two? Could go either way, with this one.

And the ring. She'd need that.

Gathering her cleaning supplies, she bounded up the stairs to prepare the tower room. No one had used it since the princess, and this time—well, this would be a first.

She opened the door and stepped into the most special room in The Depot. A jewelry box waited on the writing desk. A simple wooden one with few embellishments, save the carved magnolia on the top.

"Oh dear." She held the box. Challenge added upon challenge. Would her aging heart be up to the task? She ran a finger over the flower symbolizing a turbulent time in their nation's history. The girl would have questions and a lot of them.

Mrs. Easley hesitated before opening the box. A plain gold band gleamed inside, along with a note.

Send him to pick them up at the station.

Them?

"Oh dear." Those seemed to be the only words she had today.

Well, it wasn't for her to know all the details. She simply followed as she was led.

She pocketed the note meant only for her and put the box containing the ring back on the table. In the wardrobe, she found appropriate clothing meant for the girl. She'd need some familiar things to start the transition.

"Hoop skirts." Mrs. Easley wrinkled her nose. "I always did find these things impractical."

She closed the wardrobe and whistled to herself, getting everything in order. Once the room was ready for her gentleman guest, she returned to her suite to prepare.

The walk-in closet held clothing from every era for nearly a thousand years. She ran her hand along the selections, stopping midway through the set for the 1800s. She hadn't worn one of these giant gowns in ages. They did tend to make passing through normal doorways rather frustrating.

After more time tugging, twisting, and pulling than she would have liked, she stuffed her aging figure into the numerous layers required of a lady of the time.

She'd finished tucking the last lock of graying hair into a snood when the doorbell rang.

"Looks like our courier is here." Giving her bodice one final tug, she started down the stairs to greet the man who had to be her most daring adventurer yet.

Dear reader,

I hope you enjoyed your trip to the 1920s. If you would take a few moments to leave a sentence or two about what you enjoyed either on my author's bookshop or online wherever you purchased the book, I would greatly appreciate it. Reader reviews truly do make a difference and help me keep this writer dream going!

More Back Inn Time books are coming soon!

Keep up with the newest releases by joining my newsletter on my website.

www.StepheniaMcGee.com

Special thanks!

Thank you to all of my amazing readers who helped with the culinary aspects of this book. I appreciate y'all letting me pepper you with questions about culinary school and for your insights on professional cooking!

A special shout out to Abby Hinojos, who helped me with the language and cultural aspects of the story! Your notes were a lifesaver.

If I have misrepresented the Cuban culture in any way, I deeply apologize. It was my intention to celebrate the amazing food, family values, and rich heritage to the best of my ability.

To every reader who has taken these trips through time with me, thank you. I can't do this without you.

Books by Stephenia H. McGee

Ironwood Family Saga
The Whistle Walk
Heir of Hope
Missing Mercy

The Accidental Spy Series
*Previously published as The Liberator Series
An Accidental Spy
A Dangerous Performance
A Daring Pursuit

Stand Alone Titles
In His Eyes
Eternity Between Us
The Cedar Key
The Secrets of Emberwild
The Swindler's Daughter

Time Travel
Her Place in Time
(Stand alone, but ties to Rosswood from The Accidental Spy Series)
The Hope of Christmas Past
(Stand alone, but ties to Belmont from In His Eyes)
The Back Inn Time Series
(Stand alone books that can be read in any order)

Novellas
The Heart of Home
The Hope of Christmas Past

Buy direct from the author's online bookshop!
Support the author and find great deals.

https://shop.stepheniamcgee.com

Stephenia H. McGee is a multi-published author of stories of faith, hope, and healing set in the Deep South. She lives in Mississippi, where she is a mom of two rambunctious boys, writer, dreamer, and husband spoiler. Her novel *The Cedar Key* was a 2021 Faith, Hope, and Love Readers' Choice award winner. A member of the ACFW (American Christian Fiction Writers) and the DAR (Daughters of the American Revolution), she loves all things books and history. Stephenia also loves connecting with readers and can often be found having fun with her Faithful Readers Team on Facebook. For more on books and upcoming events and to connect with Stephenia, visit her at www.StepheniaMcGee.com

Be sure to sign up for my newsletter to get sneak peeks, behind the scenes fun, recipes, and special giveaways!

Sign up using this link and get a free eBook!
https://newsletter.stepheniamcgee.com/u9qdt7amwv

Stephenia H. McGee, Christian Fiction Author

stepheniahmcgee

Stephenia H. McGee

Buy direct from the author's online bookshop!
Support the author and find great deals.

Shop.stepheniamcgee.com